THE DRAGON IN THE STONE

BY

IAN P MARSHALL

Dedication

Hi, thank you for purchasing this book.

So many books and their authors have inspired me and triggered my imagination to try and follow in their footsteps, that it is hard to pick just a few names but some have been with me as faithful companions through my adolescence and then into adult life; that they have almost become part of my psyche. Every time one of these author's books came out, I would excitedly buy it and fall into its spell within the first few pages. I would often re-read a book and find something new in it that made it feel fresh and exciting each time. Robert E. Howard, J. R. R. Tolkien, Robert McCammon, Stephen King, Mike Mignola and Neil Gaimen are just a few, who have travelled with me in this journey of life. I thank them all for the joy, the thrill of the ride, that they have given me over the years. That joy of adventure and mystery of the unknown is always close to my heart and, I hope, has transferred into the story you are about to read.

If you are reading this, then I hope you enjoy this story as much as I enjoyed writing it. Bringing characters to life and the adventures they then face are an absolute pleasure for me to produce. I almost feel every step they take, every act they perform as if I were in their shoes, a child again, on one more great adventure.

The setting for this novel is close to my heart, so most of the places that are in this story are real and can be looked up on google. I have changed some of the place names and all the characters are fictitious - as far as I know! And if you have never visited Dartmoor, then I would recommend a visit, it is beautiful, wild, desolate and above all, magical. Yes, magical, like the earth itself you stand on is steeped in legend and ancient history. The whole atmosphere and smell of the place breathes magic. Come along and see for yourself, feel it, feel the magic of Dartmoor.

This first novel of the 'together forever' girls is just the start of more magical adventures that the young ladies will face in their future. That is, if they all survive this one first! I have a clear plan of where I want to take this series and I am very excited about putting pen to paper again, or should I say, finger to pad, so rest assured, this will not be the last you hear of Sam, Jazz and Chloe.

I would also like to thank Dave Kingdon, from Devon Proofreading, and all my family, and friends for their continual support and encouragement.

Ian P Marshall
20th April 2020

Characters, Places and Artefacts

Characters

Sam - Our inquisitive young adventurer and close friends of Jazz and Chloe.

Jazz - Long term friend of Sam and Chloe and the most authoritative.

Chloe - The last of the 'forever together' group.

Sol Constantine - Part time teacher, and Guardian of the Earth.

Percival Lamberts - An Earth Guardian and colleague of Sol's.

Moribund - Our protagonist, an evil Guardian, hell bent on restoring his order.

Lawrence Kane - Missing Guardian of the Earth.

Miss Hingstone - Teacher and friend of Sol's.

The Skree - A race of beings from the first age of man.

The Trolls - A race of stone giants who live under bridges or near running water.

Places

Dartmoor - A beautiful National Park located in the heart of Devon.

Widecombe in the Moor - A small village on Dartmoor.

Wotter – A small village on Dartmoor.

Dewerstone - The site of Devil's Rock.

Cadover - A popular destination on Dartmoor for picnickers, tourists and walkers.

Burrator Reservoir - A picturesque reservoir located on Dartmoor.

Plymouth - City on the edge of Dartmoor.

Ivybridge - A ever expanding town on the outskirts of Plymouth

that borders Dartmoor.
The Toll House Bookstore - An old toll house and home to the Guardians.

Artefacts

The Books of Time - These detail the three ages of man and hold forgotten knowledge and, hidden powers.
Excalibur- Said to be the most powerful sword of the 13 of the Knights of the Round Table.

Contents

CHAPTER 1 –A NARROW ESCAPE

CHAPTER 2 – THE JOURNAL

CHAPTER 3 – TO THE MOOR

CHAPTER 4 – THE GUARDIANS

CHAPTER 5 – MAGIC!

CHAPTER 6 – INTO DARKNESS!

CHAPTER 7 – THE RESCUE

CHAPTER 8 – TRAPPED

CHAPTER 9 –
TROLLSWORTHY WARREN

CHAPTER 10 – THE DRAGON AWAKENS

Epilogue 1

Epilogue 2

CHAPTER 1- A NARROW ESCAPE!

"Now listen closely," the man said with a deep low voice, and paused. The speaker leant forward towards the fire and his face took on a foreboding and serious look to the enrapt children sat about the flickering embers. One child sniggered, but was quickly silenced by an elbow in the ribs from the girl sitting next to him. 12 children and two adults sat around a fire that had already started to dwindle. A warm summer breeze made the flames flicker and dance in the moonlight and through the scattered cloud cover, stars twinkled joyously above the small huddled group. The light wind continued its hidden journey ruffling through the tight packed tents behind them and then silence reigned again, as if the earth itself was listening to the story that was about to be told.

"You have all heard of the legends of Dartmoor, of the hairy hands that suddenly appear and pull unsuspecting drivers off the road and to their doom, of the Devil who visited Widecombe in the Moor, only a few miles away from here, I might add. He came to collect a sinner who had made a pact with the devil over a gambling debt and lost! And nearly on this very spot, the ghostly wild hunt starts, driving all who see it across the moor and over the cliffs at the Dewerstone rock, to be dashed and swept away in the foaming river below, never to be seen again ... " Utter silence prevailed. The children's faces looked locked in stone, eyes wide, hypnotised by the power of the word and mind.

"Mr Constantine, I think that is enough," a woman's stern voice said from the other side of the fire. The man looked up, a wry smile on his face, one eyebrow raised.

"I think you are scaring the children!" she added. The spell was broken. And with a few, 'No, we're not scared' and 'Oh, please, Miss Hingstone, just one more story, please,' she relented.

"One more story and then bed, and keep it ... nicer, please, Mr Constantine."

The man opened his hands up in front of him, in submission. "As you wish." And then he continued "Let me take you back to a time forgotten from history, a time before Atlantis sank and Lemuria ruled the waves, where magnificent towered cities covered the land, a time when giants walked the earth and Dragons flew, a time when a great war raged between the armies of man and an ancient race of beings we will simply call, the lizard people. They were hell bent on wiping us off the face of the earth. For centuries the war raged until a final great battle right here on Dartmoor took place ... " Again, he paused and looked around at the group as if awaiting a question.

"Who won, who won?" a young voice blurted out.

"Well, we did, of course!" he said wistfully. "Otherwise we wouldn't be here! The great army of the lizard people were defeated, its people driven deep underground and banished to live there forever. The great creatures they had summoned, the Dragons and giants were turned to stone where they stood, and even now, if you know where to look, you can see their stone bodies scattered about the moor. In fact, literally, 10 yards from here, one of the great Dragon's heads stands ... "

"I think that is just about enough for tonight, Mr Constantine," Miss Hingstone butted in. "No more ifs and buts, please. Off to your tents, we have a lot of walking to do tomorrow and you will all need a good night's sleep."

After a few, 'ahhs', and 'ohhs', the children rose from the blankets they had been sitting on and traipsed back to their tents with a few mumbling 'good night' on the way. Out of the 12 children, three of them were girls.

One of the girls paused and looked back at the two teachers now sat together beside the dying embers of the fire, the features on their faces shimmering in the firelight.

Mr Constantine sat with his head turned to Miss Hingstone, while twiddling a large ornate gold ring on the little finger of his right hand. They seemed deep in quiet argument, as only teachers can do. The girl in question was called Samantha Burton, Sam for short. She was a tall gangly child with long straight, auburn, hair that hung to the middle of her back. A few freckles, which were more prominent at this time of year, adorned her nose and cheeks. A pair of designer glasses sat comfortably on her pretty, mousy, face. She was two weeks away from her 14th birthday, and Sam and the other year nine children were on the last day of their activity break, a week's camping upon the moor. She couldn't have had a better time if she had tried.

This had been an adventure worth waiting for. Every day had been as exciting as the last. The weather had been fantastic and everyone had got on well. Things had got even better when Mr Jones had been suddenly taken ill and the supply teacher

Mr Constantine had taken his place, at the last minute. Mr Constantine was pretty cool as they saw it. He seemed different, dressed differently and acted almost as if he was on their side, not the teachers. Despite always being deep in thought, he would break from his reverie with an instant smile and open ear. About 30 years old and with a set of unruly brown hair above his, often unshaven features,

Mr Constantine, always looked dishevelled and in a hurry. On, numerous occasions he turned up late for school, walking into the classroom with a mumbled oath and apology all thrown into one. With a strong roman nose, deep brooding eyes and striking features, Mr Sol Constantine was quite a head-turner, as Sam had noticed when the female teachers and mothers came into contact with him. With a deep, but smooth, dreamlike voice and bright sparkling blue eyes, he seemed to have the ability to control the classroom the instant he walked in. Yet somehow this week, she had noticed that he had seemed different, more distant. At times, he almost acted as if he didn't know them at all and had to concentrate to remember everyone's names.

The other two girls with Sam were the closest thing she had to friends in school. Chloe Barnes was slightly shorter and more rounded with shortish blonde hair and a gap toothed grin that sort of made everyone smile. Chloe had met Jazz Jones-Hughes, the third of the three girls, the first day of school and had pretty much been in her shadow ever since. If slavery had not been abolished, then Chloe would pretty much have been Jazz's slave! She looked up to Jazz and put her on a pedestal and did almost anything that Jazz asked without question. Jazz was the one that all the girls looked up to without even knowing it, but she was still just a little too young to realise the power she had to control the others around her. Slightly outspoken and forthright, Jazz Jones-Hughes ran the show. To Sam, though, Jazz was just a friend. Hero worship wasn't her thing. She knew Jazz was the alpha girl as the adults called it, but it didn't bother her. Yes, Jazz was the pretty one, who always made a bit more of an effort to dress up and look the best. She was always the one who got her way with a smile, a flick of her wavy blonde hair and twinkle of her blue eyes, but none of that really mattered to Sam. Jazz was just her friend, they had known each other a long time and they got on well and as far as she was concerned, that was all that mattered. Sam turned away from the teachers and entered her tent. After a few minutes, getting comfortable in their sleeping bags, the girls whispered amongst themselves over the day's events before fatigue, tired minds and bodies gave in to the clutches of the sandman. Around the packed tents of sleeping children, the wind began to rise again and dark clouds raced across the night sky blotting out whole galaxies of stars as they passed. Eventually, the wind calmed and a near full moon poked its head out from behind the dispersing clouds. A fine mist began to form in the shallow valley, hanging above the earth like a thin blanket of cloud. By now, only Mr Constantine remained beside the dwindling fire, his eyes watching the burning wood with fascination, his mind deep in thought. He reached into his jacket pocket and withdrew an old frayed journal, leather bound and held together by an old brass clasp. He opened it, flicked through a few pages and paused on one. He took out a pen and hastily scribbled something, before tying the journal up. A sound somewhere close by, out of sight from the fire-light, made him start and break his reverie. It sounded like a low rumbling coming from a few paces in front of him. His eyes narrowed as he straightened, trying to peer into the darkness. He knew that night sounds on the moor often played tricks with your senses, but nevertheless, he rose up, a frown forming on his face, as he quickly peered over his right shoulder towards Miss Hingstone's tent. All was quiet, no movement. He shrugged and a moment later, he started forward, past the dying embers of the campfire and out onto the moonlit moor, journal in hand.

After less than 50 paces, he stopped at the end of a narrow gulley. Gorse bushes and fern banked either side of the rise, casting dark shadows onto the tight cropped turf beneath his feet. In front of him, a huge boulder about 15 feet long and about four feet wide, blocked his passage. It jutted out of the earth to nearly six feet, his entire height. Behind and to his right, the rock levelled off with the top of the rise, but from where he was standing, it was an impressive and foreboding sight. Moonlight shone off the top of the grey stone and moss covered it, in places, showing up as dark patches. Anyone with even a small bit of imagination could see the long angular Dragon head shape he had described earlier to the children. Other boulders could be seen strewn about the gulley, barely visible above the tops of the ferns.

Sol knew the noise had come from this direction and a feeling of unease began to gnaw at his thoughts. The temperature had suddenly dropped, and his breath hung in the air in front of him causing him to shiver and he instinctively wrapped his coat closer about his lean frame. He looked at the rock again; the closest side to him completely enshrouded in shadow, and something about it looked wrong. With the knowledge he possessed, fear began to creep across his features. He reached the rock, knelt and felt along the base where it joined the earth.

"No!" he said in utter horror and waded through the ferns to his right and then clambered up onto the rock itself. With an urgency no one had ever seen in him before, he opened the journal in his hand, but cursed when he realised that the light was too bad to read what was within. He stood atop the rock, looking back towards the tents as if in fear for the ones that slept, that knew nothing of the real reason he was here. His shadow from the moon cast a long dark line along the valley floor. He heard the bleating of sheep in the distance and from his vantage point, the faint light in the sky of the city of Plymouth could clearly be seen in the night sky. The mist covered the earth in a dense layer of thin white fog, hanging there like a field of cotton, giving him the feeling that he was marooned on a desert island. And then the earth beneath his feet suddenly gave way, the solid rock split asunder with a crack and he tumbled down into the gap created by the split. His journal dropped from shocked hands, bounced once off the side of the rock then fell to the valley floor, as he reached out to grasp the edge of the rock and was successful. With eyes wide, he started to pull himself up and out of the widening chasm. He kicked out with his feet to find purchase and found little. "Not now!" he shouted above the din of the rendering rock.

"Not now, please?" he pleaded as he pulled his head above the rim and managed to get one elbow over the top to give himself leverage to lift himself out. And just when he thought he was pulling himself free, something that felt like a tentacle, long, cold and sinuous, wrapped itself around one leg and then the other. He made one long agonising shriek and then was gone, his cries diminishing as even more tentacles wrapped themselves around his form, drawing him down into the pitch blackness of the earth. The rock began to reform, leaving no trace of the man, or the deed that had transpired only moments before. Only the journal lying on the ground a few metres from the rock, gave away any clue that something was amiss.

Sam awoke with a start! Was that thunder she had heard. Something had woken her. Always a light sleeper, Sam knew it could have been anything, but was sure she had heard something loud! Her two friends were still fast asleep, and she thought about waking them, but decided she would just be made to look silly.

Climbing out of her sleeping bag, she tossed on some clothes and quietly as possible unzipped the tent, stepped out, and then zipped it back up again. The cold gripped her face instantly and she shivered despite the warmth of her clothes.

Tucking her hands into pockets, she noticed that a few embers, of the fire were still glowing red. The quiet of the night was almost tangible, no roar of thunder sounded, until a distant human shriek of utter horror shattered the silence. Instinctively, she knew that voice! Mr Constantine! And before she knew it, she was pacing forwards, towards where she thought the scream came from, her feet hardly making a sound on the soft moorland turf and muffled by the thin blanket of mist. Moonlight led her instinctively to the end of the valley, where she halted in front of a large stone. Nothing moved and Sam suddenly realised what a stupid thing she had done! What was she thinking? Was she mad? Why didn't she try and wake Miss Hingstone?

She turned to run back to the tents, when her foot caught something on the floor.She reached down and picked up the journal and recognised it immediately as

Mr Constantine's. He had this on him at all times. It never left his sight and he was always overly protective towards it. So where was Mr Constantine, she thought?

Behind her, from a fissure in the rock, eight silent black tendrils began to form into solid tentacles that swirled and writhed and then began to head towards her in unison, sliding over the rock like snakes. Sam flicked open the journal, then quickly shut it again. It wasn't for her to look at, she thought, just as the first tentacle wrapped itself around her ankle and jerked her off her feet, knocking her face first onto the turf. The wind was knocked out of her and her scream of fear came out like a whimper, making hardly a sound. Her eyes wide and shaking in fright, she turned on to her backside and instinctively kicked out at the thing grasping her leg, as four more tentacles attached themselves.

Above her the rock began to open again, just as her feet touched the bottom of the stone. And then something came out of the fissure, not something, a human hand and arm, grasping the tentacles and pulling them back with such incredible force that it actually made them lose their hold upon the young girl. Sam thought she heard a distant voice, saying "Not tonight you don't." And then suddenly she was free.

Sam leapt to her feet, grabbing the journal as she rose and started running back towards camp with a realisation that in the moonlight, she had glimpsed upon the little finger of the hand, a large gold ring.

Over her shoulder, she glimpsed the tentacles reaching out for her again, but she was too fast and in seconds she was out of their reach. They quickly withdrew and to her utter astonishment, disappeared back into the rock. The silence that followed was almost more horrific.

Panic and fear gripped her in a vice of steel that made breathing difficult. How could she explain what she had seen, what had happened to her? Would anyone believe that

Mr Constantine had been dragged down into the earth and that had it not been for him, she would have met the same fate! Sobbing and shaking, she made her way to her tent, unzipped it and literally threw herself in, before zipping it up, as if the action of it formed a solid barrier that made her safe. She knew the thought was silly, but it helped. She tucked the journal into her back pack and curled up into a ball atop her sleeping bag, nervous exhaustion and fear, enough to send her into a fitful sleep.

* * *

At the other end of the valley, the stone once more split asunder with a resounding screech of solid rock being forced apart. A dark and sinuous form erupted out of the fissure, rolling off the top of the rock to end up crashing into the ferns and gorse behind the large stone. The fissure slammed shut with a clunk, as something moved within the knee-high vegetation.

A cocoon like form rippled with a creaking of bones and knotting of muscle. A moment's silence then the translucent cocoon ripped and frayed as something inside forced its way out. A human figure emerged.

CHAPTER 2 - THE JOURNAL

Sam woke again with the sound of raised voices outside her tent and was instantly aware of what had transpired the night before. She shot up with a start and looked about her, her heart racing, knowing that outside someone had probably been reported missing and only she knew the truth. Guilt lay heavy on her conscience. Why hadn't she done anything. Subconsciously she reached down and rubbed her calf and realised with a fright, it was sore from where the tentacle had attached itself to her. She shuddered, snatching her hand away and straightened up, a shiver going down her spine. She bent down again, pulled up her trouser leg and stared at the marks upon her leg. Her hand went to her mouth to stifle a scream. The marks were like a two inch, burn line and the way it had wrapped itself around the leg was obvious to see.

The other two were stirring beside her and she realised suddenly that she was still dressed from her night's excursion. She hopped to her feet, quietly unzipped and then more loudly, zipped up the sleeping bag. Brushing herself down, she made a deliberate yawn and stretch, calling to the others to wake up. Should she have woken them in the night and told them what happened?

If she had, at least she would have had someone to stand beside her. But would they have believed her, if she had? She stared at the unopened tent, putting off the inevitable for as long as possible.

Sam looked at her hands and saw that they were shaking, and then seeing that the others were still only just stirring, she took a deep breath and made her way outside. Sunlight made her raise her hand to her forehead to shield herself from the brightness. She glimpsed figures around a newly lit fire and smelt the wonderful odour of bacon cooking, even before she heard the hissing of the fat in the pan.

Two of the boys, John Gammon, a large boy with a round face and eyes inset into his face that made him look like he was squinting, and Harry Taylor, his best friend, a rather tall thin lad with jet black hair; were arguing outside their tent about who was going to take the tent down today! 'Every day!' Sam thought, shaking her head! 'Every day they argued over who was going to take the tent down! Boys!'

And then she stopped dead in her tracks, her thoughts dissolved in an instant as she stared, open eyed, at the person holding the frying pan in one hand and a fork in the other, Mr Constantine! Her mouth dropped open and her legs stopped moving, a huge sense of relief coursing through her.

Gathering herself with a smile, she was about to step forwards when a pair of hands grabbed her waist, while at the same time, a shout of "boo" and some giggling, made her jump in fright so much, she felt like she had left her shadow behind. Chloe and Jazz joined her, still laughing at the scare. "Looked like you had seen a ghost before we scared you," said Jazz, putting her arm around Sam's shoulder. Sam looked to the heavens and smiled. "You don't know the half of it!" she said, almost to herself.

By now, they had reached the fire with breakfast being prepared, and for the first time, Sam took a closer look at Mr Constantine. To Sam, much to her amazement,

Mr Constantine looked absolutely fine, almost as if last night had not happened at all. He even wore the same clothes he had been wearing the previous evening.

And then she noticed something strange, something that began to form a tiny chink of doubt in her already frayed mind. Mr Constantine was no longer wearing his ring. He always wore that ring. And now, suddenly, it was gone, and especially after what had transpired last night, it gave her a strange feeling; as if something was still not right.

And then she raised her eyes to meet those of the supply teacher and her heart missed a beat, she felt a roaring in her ears, and then

suddenly she felt herself falling. She felt hands catching her and shepherding her to the floor, her only thoughts as she drifted off into fainted oblivion was that, despite the fact that Mr Constantine's eyes looked the same, some inner sense, told her that they were not, and that in fact, Mr Constantine was not
Mr Constantine at all, but some sinister imposter!

Her first feeling of consciousness was the touch of a warm hand on her forehead. Sam opened her eyes and automatically started to rise, but seeing the worried look in her mother's brown eyes, she resisted the urge and rested her head back on the pillow. She was in her bedroom, in her bed. And before she could raise any more thoughts, her mother's mind reading skills interrupted the process.
"You gave us quite a scare young lady," she said with a motherly, eyebrows raised, smile. "The doctor has been and gone, and says you passed out because you just overdid it a bit. And guess what?"
"What?" Sam replied, not quite sure whether she was going to like the answer or not. "Guess how you got here?"
"Mumm!" Sam lengthened the word into a question.
"And guess who missed it all?"
"Mummmm!"
"Starts with A and finishes with E, and sounds like semblance!"
Sam giggled, feeling fine and rose to drink a glass of water her mother was handing to her. She couldn't believe she had missed the ambulance ride!
"How are you feeling, hon?"
"I feel absolutely fine, thanks mum. Bit tired."
"Good, you look OK. What's the last thing you remember?" And then everything came back to her, everything reenacting itself, in her head, as if it was a repeat afternoon matinee at the local theatre.
"Sam, Sam, are you OK?" her mother said worriedly. "You suddenly went very pale? Did something happen out there? You can tell me, you know, if anything happened out there, you know

that, don't you?"

"Yes, of course, Mum. Nothing happened, I'm just a little tired ... and a bit embarrassed, to be honest."

"I understand, it's nothing to be ashamed of, it could happen to anyone. Knowing you, you probably haven't drunk enough water again," she said, raising her eyebrows again and shaking her head. "Now, settle down and get some rest, your friends are on the way, so don't overdo it. I'll bring some tea up later, you can have an early night, and tomorrow is the weekend, so you can chill out and take it easy, OK?"

"Yes, Mum," she replied. "Oh, Mum, did they bring all my stuff back?"

"Of course, that nice man, the supply teacher Mr Constantine, dropped it all back this afternoon. Some stuff is in the wash and the rest is at the bottom of your bed."

Fear gripped Sam in its claustrophobic embrace again, but somehow she managed to hide it from her mother this time.

"Mr Constantine was here? In the house?"

"Well he didn't post it here, did he? Yes, of course he was here. He was very polite and quite worried about you, you know."

"I'm sure he was," Sam answered under her breath.

Sam's Mum left the room with a frown on her face and a reminder to her to rest, but before she had even reached the bottom of the stairs, Sam was out of bed and rifling through her belongings from the activity week to find the journal. 'Nooo!', she thought to herself, throwing the last piece of clothing back on the pile. Gone! The journal was gone! Now what was she going to do. It was her only piece of solid evidence to last night's events.

"You're not looking for this, by any chance?" a young well-spoken voice said from behind her. Sam turned to see Jazz standing there, waving the journal in her right hand, a broad smile on her pretty face.

Chloe stood behind and to her right. "Good to see you are OK."

For a second, they all stood still, then the three girls smiled broadly, raised their voices in a scream of delight and hugged each other as if they hadn't seen each other in years.

Jazz broke away first, brushing herself down and tinkering with her clothes to make sure she looked perfect, before turning back to Sam, with a pensive look on her face. "Now are you going to tell us, why you had this with you, or do we need to somehow get it back to Mr Constantine without him knowing, no questions asked?"

Sam sat down on the end of the bed and took a deep long sigh. "You know you're not going to believe this, but here goes!" and Sam told them everything.

They sat in silence for a few seconds when she had finished, Jazz shaking her head as if she was trying to rid herself of the words she had heard, while Chloe sat cross legged on a rug, with a frown in open-mouthed amazement. At the end, she rolled up her pyjama bottom to show them her leg, but the marks had gone, not a sign remained. She looked at them incredulously and was momentarily speechless, her eyes wide in disbelief.

"For once, I really don't know what to say," Jazz stammered, her practical mind struggling to deal with something so out of the ordinary.

"That makes a change," Sam replied, trying to break the ice.

"But I do believe something happened to you, so whatever you are up to, we're in, right Chloe."

"Of course, we are a team, now and forever, together forever, remember."

"Now and forever, together forever," the other two replied in unison, causing another outburst of giggling.

'Now and forever, together forever' had become their pact, a simple motto, stating that they would always be there for each other, whatever and whenever. And this was definitely a 'whatever and whenever' situation.

"So, what next?" Chloe asked.

"Perhaps the diary will give you some clues?" Jazz said, passing it to Sam.

Sam peered down at the book, feeling the weight of the thing and the feel of the old parched leather in her hand. It felt warm to the touch and looked incredibly old. Certain pages seemed to have escaped somewhat, causing the book to look a little dishevelled, but still orderly. A small brass clasp held everything together, and this, she flicked open, while the other two girls huddled up close behind her, one peering over either shoulder. The journal fell open on her lap and she looked around anxiously knowing that she, they, were crossing a line that would be hard to turn back from.

The first thing she noticed was that even the paper seemed old and frail, almost brittle to the touch. The book had fallen open close to the middle. They noticed a scrawling flowing script, interspersed with dates, a small simple drawing and some symbols that looked like nothing they had seen before.

At first, the pencilled drawing made Sam draw her breath in with a gasp. The basic sketch was of a stone upon the moor, which for a moment, she thought was the same one from the night before, but on closer inspection, she realised that it was not. A small inscription read 'Dagon's Mound'. And then in what looked like a hurried scribbled pencil beside it, 'at least six inches'.

For some unknown reason, Sam flicked through the pages until she got to the last two, and this time she did gasp. Another pencilled drawing, this one clearly a sketch of the stone from the previous night, with an inscription beneath which said 'The Dragon's Head'.

Starting with a date, there followed a lot more scribbled text in almost diary format, and the urgency in the writing was clear to be seen by all.

14th June 2012

It seems that I am too late! The Dragon is rising! Something has happened. The Morn stones have failed. The magic is failing! We have been complacent. I pray that we are not too late. Lawrence was right all along. If only he was here now, he would know what to do ...'

And then it finished.
Sam flicked the pages back to the inside cover and a letter fell out

onto the bed. She opened and it was addressed to a *Mr P Lamberts,* *'The Old Toll House, Ivybridge, Devon PL21 …'*
She looked at it, for a moment, then began reading aloud.

"Dear Percival,
Apologies for not being in touch for a while, but I am now closer than ever to finding what we need. I know Soloman doesn't believe, but my instincts tell me otherwise. The book always predicts the truth despite its ambiguous nature. We ARE nearing the third age of man. I know Soloman doesn't agree, but he will on my return. And, yes, with grace, I will return soon.
Live well, my friend.
Yours,
Lawrence"

She refolded the letter and placed it back in the book. The inside of the front cover was full of more strange writing and glyphs. She noticed that the new scribbles were different from the text throughout the rest of the journal, making her feel that two different people had been working on it.
"I don't get any of that!" Chloe retorted.
"What does that mean?" Jazz asked, ignoring Chloe. "That bit about the magic. It almost sounds like a warning! And they talk as if magic is real? As if?" she added with a sigh.
Sam remained silent, deep in thought, flicking back through the pages and stopping at any one that had sketches of rocks. "Look!" she said, pointing to a picture and then to another on a different page. "Each picture has pencilled dimensions written across them, as if he was measuring something! But what? What was he so afraid of? The Dragon is rising! What is that meant to mean? And who is this Lawrence Kane?" Sam paused, placed the journal on her lap and put her arms around her two friends.
"There is only one way to find out," she said with a big grin. "We are going to take a bike ride to the moor tomorrow, back to the Dragon's headstone, to see if we can spot anything in the daylight."

"Won't that be dangerous?" Chloe asked. "After what happened to you?"

"I'm guessing we will be safe in the daylight!"

"Oh, so we are a specialist on the occult now, are we?" Jazz asked with a hint of sarcasm and a twinkle in her eye.

"We will find out tomorrow, won't we?"

"I'm in," Chloe said. "Sounds like fun!"

"Oh, God give me strength! OK, a bike ride it is then."

And with that, the adventure of their lifetime was set in motion.

CHAPTER 3 - TO THE MOOR

The sun was already out when Sam told her mum she was going to ride over to Jazz's to keep her company on a trip to Exeter, that her parents had planned. It was a normal occurrence, as they were inseparable, and Jazz's house was only 10 minutes away, but after what had transpired, her mother was a little reluctant to let her go.

Sam felt guilty about telling a white lie to her mum, it was something that she never did and it felt uncomfortable telling her that they were going to Exeter.

Over a full cooked breakfast, Sam explained that she felt fine and had just overdone it. While eating, her eyes and ears turned to the local news broadcaster on the television, interviewing someone about the unexplained reason why Burrator Reservoir was near to overflowing, despite all attempts to control the levels. 'Boring,' she thought and turned her attention to her Mum, and with some gentle persuasion and a big hug, she was shortly on her way cycling down the lane to her friend's house, backpack on and journal safely tucked inside.

But instead of turning right, she turned left and headed on up the road that took her to Dartmoor. A moment later, she heard the joint tinkle of bike bells. Coming up a lane adjacent to her were her two friends, helmets on, young legs out of the saddle, both pumping hard to reach Sam first. Chloe got there just ahead of Jazz, who on arrival ignored the fact and carried on talking.

"Fancy seeing you here!"

"Nice day." Sam said, breathing hard. Sam felt tired, her normal sleep had been interrupted by nightmarish visions of Dragons and lizard men advancing en masse across the moor, red eyes glowing in the dark, and she had woken herself twice in the night, sweating and shaking in fear, before eventually nodding off again.

"Good day for an adventure!" Chloe replied. "First to the grid wins." she said and was gone like the wind.

The 'grid' was the cattle grid that defined the start of the moor. The change in the land from fertile fields to moorland was instant and amazing to see and the cattle grids denoted where the moorland started, but also helped keep the native livestock on the moor. Half an hour from there and they would be at Cadover Bridge and minutes from where they had been camping below Wigford Down.

Without even a backwards look, Jazz pushed down on her pedals and started off, leaving Sam and Chloe to catch up. With back packs on and the warmth of the sun on their backs, the going was tough, as the route up to the moor was a long slow climb that soon tested their young legs and lungs.

A light warm breeze ruffled their hair as they passed a busy riding stable, then passed through some overhanging trees and, for a short while, into the shadows and, thankfully, out of the sun. The sounds and smell of the country was all around them, and a freshness to the air was almost tangible. Sam clicked her gears back to the lowest possible and pedalled within herself, looking ahead at her two friends.

Was she leading them into danger? What happened if something happened to one of them? What were they expecting to find? And why did none of them want to talk about

Mr Constantine?

They had already crossed the cattle grid a mile back, beside a fast-flowing small river that swept off the moor with great purpose, as if the water itself was in a hurry to reach the sea. Newly shorn sheep dotted the grassy curb, and because of the newness of the day, some sheep were still lying asleep on the road itself, oblivious to motorist and cyclist alike! These they gave a wide berth to, with a shout of 'sheep alert' from Chloe, as if she was the lookout on the Titanic, shouting 'iceberg ahead'.

By now, the road had levelled off and the girls drew level with each other, just as they neared the giant quarries of the clay pits. Huge sections of the earth had been cut from the moor, as if chiselled by some enormous knife, exposing the white clay that was so sought after. Water, azure blue in colour, lay at the bottom of some of the pits, and some hardy sheep, like mountain goats, clung to the artificial hills, looking for food, seemingly unaware of their predicament. The hills themselves looked like giant pyramids with their tops cut off. A lonely tree, clung to the slopes, its branches hard and gnarled, its features bent away from the prevailing winds.

Sam had rallied her energy and was feeling a lot livelier now. The cycling was easy going, the day was just perfect and she was with her best friends. What could possibly go wrong? To her left, the view of Plymouth and beyond to the breakwater and sea was absolutely stunning. They had been this way many times and every time it took her breath away. She knew that if she mentioned it to the others though, they wouldn't understand, so she just enjoyed the view for herself.

Cars passed on a regular basis and all seemed so normal, so much so, that for the first time she questioned her own mind. She reached back behind her to feel the shape of the journal to reassure her.

Passing Wotter, they now reached the open moor itself where gorse clung to the moorland in places, interspersed with fern. Horses, ponies, cows and sheep dotted the rolling countryside, nibbling at the tight grass or lying down, basking in the sunlight. There was a calmness and also at the same time a bleakness about the moor that Sam loved, and despite the recent events, she felt very much at home there.

Since childhood, she had been letterboxing or coming up in the dead of winter when snow was on the ground, toboggan at the ready. Many times, she had climbed the local tors, finding new ways to the tops every time. It was a dangerous place, especially when the fog came down or the weather suddenly changed, it could become a very scary, foreboding and dark place. To Sam, she related it to the sea, beautiful, ever changing, but dangerous, a thing to always respect and never take for granted.

Cadover Bridge came into sight over a rise, a popular place for locals and visitors alike. The car park was already filling, families were setting up tents and picnic areas along the beautiful fast flowing river Plym. The river itself was littered in places with giant boulders, that broke the flow, causing eddies and mini rapids.

A group of kids in wet suits were already lining up to jump off the bridge into a deep part of the river, beneath the bridge. Sam felt herself tense instinctively, as her gaze rose above Cadover Bridge towards where they had camped.

As they grew closer, everything seemed so unreal to her. Families were enjoying their day on Dartmoor, as people had done for many years, completely oblivious to the dangers, possibly, lurking beneath the earth. Could she really have seen what she thought she had?

Before she knew it, they were over the bridge and pulling the bikes off the road and into a small grassy car park. Sam felt her heart beginning to beat faster. She took some deep breaths and put on the best smile she could, for her two friends.

The first thing she noticed when she dismounted and started pushing the bike across the uneven ground, was that the large stone cross that they had camped near was now lying upturned on the moorland. The stone plinth that it had been set upon had also been pulled half out of the earth, forming a new hole filled with fresh earth.

"Wow! I wonder who did that?" Chloe exclaimed.

"I don't care; I think they are ugly anyway'" Jazz replied and moved on

"Ugly! They are beautiful and ancient and should be looked after, not vandalised," Sam retorted.

"Whatever!" came the reply.

Chloe looked at Sam and raised her eyes in silent acknowledgement. Sam stayed looking at the cross, disturbed by the scene before her. 'Had it been vandals or something worse perhaps? How come, after so many hundreds of years that the cross has stood, should it fall now,' she thought to herself?

The sound of, "Come on, Dolly Daydream," broke her reverie and she turned, pushing the bike away from the cross, towards where they had camped.

Only a small stone circle and some burnt grass within, gave away any evidence that they had camped there a few nights ago. Instinctively their gaze drifted up the tiny valley towards the Dragon head shaped stone.

Placing their bikes down, they huddled closer together, instinctively, without even knowing it and stepped onto the path between the ferns. Sam suddenly felt the silence around the tiny valley. As soon as they drew closer towards the stone, it seemed that all outside noise was muffled, as if they were in a vacuum. She could hear her own pulse beating in her temple. No birds sounded and not even an insect moved. Across the line of ferns and gorse along the valley, the top of the stone could be glimpsed, grey against the green.

The girls eyes met as they paused, a sense of fear etched across their young faces, and then suddenly something came pounding towards them out of the ferns, making them shriek in fright and then again in nervous relief as a sheep ran past them bleating and scampering away as fast as its legs could take it.

The ice was broken and they stood there huddled together, laughing and shaking their heads in amazement at how tense they had been. Overactive minds had leapt ahead, but a bleating sheep had returned them to reality, even if it had made them jump a little.

They reached the open ground between the ferns and stood looking at the huge stone before them. Sunlight glinted off the top, dazzling their eyes, but it somehow looked tarnished or dull, as if the rock itself was drawing in the power of the sun, filtering the reflection it gave off.

"Looks just like a big rock to me!" Chloe said, striding forward, unafraid or unbelieving of her friend's story. "Maybe even a bit like one of my teeth!" she continued, turning her head and putting a finger in her mouth, to stretch her cheek and show a missing tooth.

"It does actually look a bit like a Dragon's head, to be honest." Jazz nodded in agreement, looking at Sam. "But it does look much more like a piece of Dartmoor granite, though."

"Oh, God give me strength, didn't you believe anything I said?" Sam moved forward to catch up with the others. "Please be careful, I wouldn't know what to say to your parents if anything happened to you."

"Oh, that's great, don't worry about us, worry about what my folks would do!" Jazz replied jokingly. "That's just great!"

By now, Chloe had reached the rock and was starting to climb it, almost hopping and jumping, so that in seconds, she had reached the top. "See, it's just a rock!" she said jumping up and down on it like a trampoline.

"Chloe, be careful, please!" Sam said in fear, reaching the base of the rock. She looked properly at it for the first time in daylight, but didn't touch it. Moss covered the rock in many places, especially where the eyes would be, giving off the feeling that they were real eye sockets. Discoloured marks covered the rock giving it a mottled effect.

Tentatively, she reached out and touched it, unsure of what to expect. Nothing! Just cold hard rock. Perhaps it only happens at night? She was standing in the overhang of the rock now, Jazz had moved off through the ferns to reach the top without having to climb, when suddenly from around the left side of the stone, a tall silhouetted figure appeared, making Sam shriek in fear.

Despite the fact that the features were in shade and before she had even lifted her hand to shield her eyes, she knew who it was.

"Mr Constantine!" she exclaimed overly loudly, to warn her friends.

The figure stopped, seemingly taken aback at the sight of the girl in front of him. But then, after a moment to compose himself, he spoke. "Sam!" he replied with a forced smile. "What brings you up here?"

'I might ask the same of you!' She was going to say, but thought better of it. He was still her teacher after all! "I'm ..." she said stammering. Fear gripped her again, her body tensed to flee, but her feet wouldn't move and her eyes wouldn't leave the figure in front of her, as if hypnotised by the form silhouetted in front of the sun. Before she could muster a word or form a sentence of worth, Chloe came to her rescue. "Hello, Mr Constantine." she said from atop the rock. "How's it going, Sir?"

The figure turned to peer at Chloe and something about the way he moved made Sam tense again. He moved almost robotically, as if he had a really stiff neck! His body turned awkwardly to stare upwards and despite the sun, he did not even try to shield himself from it, almost as if it did not exist. No raised hand, nothing. Or was he just getting used to his human form, she thought, feeling the small hairs on her forearms rise.

And then a thought came to her, one that wanted to make her scream and run and hide all in one moment. Did this thing that was Mr Constantine, because for some reason she knew that this was not him, did he know that it was her who had seen the real Mr Constantine swallowed up by the earth?

"Hi Sir," Jazz said appearing beside Chloe, thankfully breaking her dark thoughts.

"Well, if it isn't the famous three," he said in jest. "Or have you brought the whole class?" he asked, looking around.

"No, just us." Chloe blurted out, followed by a poke in the ribs from Jazz.

"Well, I'm just on my way now. We all left in a bit of a rush the other day, and I just wanted to check that we had left the place as it should be. I'll see you girls back at school. You take care and ... be good. Oh, and Sam ..." he paused, looking back a Sam with those piercing eyes. 'What was he going to say' she thought, feeling her beating heart pounding, like a drum, in her ears.

"I hope you are feeling better now, it is a bit of a surprise to see you up and about so soon. I hope your mother knows you are up here!" Somehow, she managed to blabber out. "I'm feeling absolutely fine now, thank you, Sir. Mum thought a nice bike ride with my friends might do me good." The lie sounded hollow and she internally kicked herself for making up such a pathetic pretence.

"Bye, girls." he said walking through the ferns, over the rise and out of sight.

They stood there in silence, until they heard a car start up and drive off, and then they all let out a huge breath they didn't even know they had been holding, followed by a whistle of exclamation from Chloe.

"That was close," Jazz said. "You OK, Sam?"

"That wasn't Mr Constantine!" she said, looking up sternly at her two friends. "Or if it was, something has happened to him, something bad!"

"Woah, Woah, Woah, hold on a minute," Jazz retorted. "We all just saw him and spoke to him. It looked like him and sounded like him!" Sam was about to reply, when Chloe, who had disappeared off the back of the rock, shouted.

"Hey, guys, look what I have found!" Sam moved around the left-hand edge of the stone from where Mr Constantine had appeared and stopped. Barely 20 paces behind the rock, a dense row of gorse littered the tiny valley. The yellow buds were just coming out giving the gorse a beautiful contrast of colours between the dark green and opposing bright yellow.

Something was clinging to the needles of some of the nearest bushes, flapping in the slight breeze. At first, to Sam, it almost looked like a perished Tesco's bag, or 'Witches' Knickers' as they call them in Devon, but as she neared Chloe, who was standing next to a bush with part of it in her hand, she realised that it was something else altogether.

"Cool! Looks like snake's skin." Chloe said, holding a piece as big as her palm, up to the light. Translucent in appearance, and incredibly thin and pliable with distinct scale markings, it did look similar to an adder skin that Sam had found in her garden beneath the log box, but this was much much bigger! It was definitely a skin of sorts and it looked like it had been shed, but by whom or what?

"I am not touching that for all the money in China." Jazz said disgustedly.

"Tea!" Sam replied, not taking her eyes off the skin. "Tea in China." she reached out and plucked off a piece over a foot and a half long and about eight inches in diameter. She looked from that to the line of gorse and all the other pieces flickering in the wind like silver fish. Another thought entered her mind and started to form a picture, something about the story that the real Mr Constantine had told on the night of his disappearance about a race of lizard people, but she quickly shook her head and told herself off, banishing the scary thought to the recycle bin.

"Must have been a big snake!" she said with a voice that didn't sound like hers. Sam folded and put the sample in her rucksack, then turned back to her friends.

Jazz frowned. "I didn't know there were any big snakes on the moor or even in the UK."

"There aren't!" Sam said quietly.

"Perhaps it escaped from a zoo or a private home nearby?" Chloe added.

"I'll look it up on the iPad when I get home. Now let's go look at that rock." A few paces took them back to the rock. With reluctance she stood atop of it and looked at it from every angle possible, but nothing looked out of the ordinary. Dejectedly, they all sat down for a drink and rest. Chloe sat with her back to the rock while Jazz found a suitable one nearby to relax and sun herself. Sam sat on a tuft of grass looking a bit forlorn, a bottle of water in one hand, the journal in the other.

"It doesn't make sense. He talks about measurements, but I don't get it." Sam looked Chloe in the eye, who shrugged and placed her drink on the ground. The sunlight caught the bottle and a small beam of light hit the shadowed underneath of the rock, where it came out of the earth. A clear line about eight inches up the rock could be seen, like a tide mark! Sam dropped her bottle, mouth agape.

"Chloe, you are a genius." she said clambering to her feet to take a closer look.

"I am!" Chloe questioned. "Of course, I am!"

Now that she knew where to look, it was easy to see. She followed the 'tideline' around the rock to the sunlit side, covered by some ferns. Pulling the ferns aside, in haste, she found the same marks!

'The rock has lifted or perhaps risen' she thought, might be a better word. Her mind was racing now. Here was evidence, proper evidence that something was amiss. She returned to the other side of the rock to see the other two standing staring at her in amazement.

"Well, don't you see? The rock has moved, the stone has risen by about eight inches! There's the proof!"

"Proof of what?" Jazz asked, hands on hips.

"That … that … that something strange is going on around here. I don't expect you to believe me, just humour me, please?"

"We're here, aren't we?"

"Yes, of course, thank you."

"So, what next?" Chloe asked.

"I think it's time we visited The Old Toll House, don't you?"

"What are we, detectives now." Jazz said, looking at the nails on her right hand, checking for any imperfections.

"Exactly." Sam said with more confidence than she felt!

CHAPTER 4 - THE GUARDIANS

Sam pressed the doorbell and involuntarily took a step back and nearly knocked her two friends over. Inside she heard the faint sound of an antique bell, followed by some movement from within.

While she waited for the footsteps to approach, she looked over the outside of the house. It was now mid-afternoon, the sun was high in the sky, and they had decided after a quick packed lunch, to head directly towards Ivybridge to find the Old Toll house.

An almost superstitious dread had seized them when taking a short cut across the moor, they had come across another up-turned cross. Even Jazz had kept silent at this discovery, as she too felt that something sinister was amiss. They had cycled past it almost in slow motion, looking at the cross that had been standing for centuries, through countless wars and some of the worst weather imaginable, unmoving and resolute in the face of everything thrown at it, until now. What had disturbed this cross and the one by the campsite was no act of human vandalism! Something else, something beneath the earth was upturning these crosses, but why? Sam couldn't answer this, but she thought that perhaps the person she was about to meet, might just be able to help.

The house was the typical shape of a toll house from olden days, that were positioned on all of the most popular roads in the late 18th and19th century, to exact a toll from travellers passing through, rather like the Tamar Bridge nowadays, she thought. The house was still close to a road but it was a minor one, hardly used now the bypass had been built. The building was painted white and was hexagonal in shape. A large oak front door stood before them, as they waited with baited breath. The footsteps neared and stopped. Nothing happened.

The girls looked at each other and raised their palms to the sky. Sam sighed, feeling that time was against them, then proceeded to knock with her knuckles on the door itself.

"What do you want?" came a short sharp reply. The voice sounded agitated.

"Er … hello, hi, we are from Mr Constantine's school, we are in his class. I'm here with a couple of my friends. We would like to speak to you if possible."

"Go away. I'm not in the mood for speaking, I am indisposed."

"Something happened to me on the moor. I saw something," Sam stammered out quickly. There was silence for a few seconds, as everyone seemed to hold their breaths. A floorboard creaked within.

"Go away, I say."

"We have just ridden here from Wigford Down," Sam continued on.

"I don't care! Go away, go away, go away, leave me alone," said the voice.

Sam had had enough. "Sol Constantine?" she said aloud.

"What about him?" came the quick reply.

"Something has happened to him, something bad!"

Again silence, but then a few moments later they heard the turning of the key in a lock and the pulling back of a deadlock. The door swung inwards with a slight creak and there standing before them was an old man of about 60 with a thin wiry frame, a long roman nose that sat proudly upon his angular face and balding head, where a few wisps of grey hung on for dear life. Upon his nose sat some gold reading glasses, with which he peered over at the girls, through deep set brown eyes and with a large frown above his bushy greying eyebrows. The man wore a tan coloured three-piece, matching, tweed suit that looked like it had seen better days.

"What type of something bad?" he asked in a strangely but familiar youthful voice, which the man raised his own eyes at.

"He's been taken!"

"Taken? By who?" the voice changed, lower in sound and tone, but somewhat forced. Sam hesitated, looking at her two friends. Chloe nodded silently.

"Something under the moor."

The man's mouth hung agape as he looked at the three girls, then he lowered his head, let out a deep sigh and said "I think you had better come in."

The door led directly into a lounge come study. Book covered shelves adorned all the walls apart from the one where a fireplace took centre stage. Above the fireplace, Sam noticed a large picture of the moor detailing a part of the moor, she did not recognise, but was somehow familiar, where a cairn of stones sat atop one of the highest points. An old-fashioned bird cage hung beside a spiral staircase, it's door open.

"Sit down, please, you are safe here," the man said. There were a single seater and double seater settee surrounding the fire place. Sam stayed still and motioned for the old man to sit.

"Thank you, Sam, but I prefer to stand. You sit down if you wish."

Sam stopped dead in her tracks. "You called me Sam? How did you know my name?" The man smiled and leant against a small dining room table. "I know all your names, Jazz, Chloe and of course yourself," he said, pointing to each one in turn. His voice was different now and familiar, but Sam could not place it.

"How? We've never met?"

"Well actually, we have ... sort of ... well, nearly ... well, we have," he mumbled, pulling a grimace.

"OK, explain?" Jazz said a little flustered. The man straightened up.

"OK, here goes. I'm Sol Constantine. I am your supply teacher at the school, Ivydene College and that is how I know you!"

"You don't look anything like, Mr Constantine. What are you talking about?" Chloe questioned.

"No, of course I don't look anything like him. That's because I am in somebody else's body. Percival Lamberts to be precise."

"Oh well, that explains it then," Jazz said with a large hint of sarcasm.

Sam looked closer at the man for some sign of jest, but he seemed to believe in what he said, there was no hint of joviality about it. In fact, the man, Percival Lamberts, he had called himself, could not have looked more serious.

"Prove it?" she asked.

And then to all the girls' amazement, he recounted a list of incidents that had taken place at school when Sol Constantine had been on supply duty, that only he could have known. The girls looked at each other, mouths agape, then at the old man and then back at each other. A black cat suddenly landed on the armrest, next to Chloe and she screamed a single high-pitched scream in shock. The cat sprang off and shot up a spiral staircase to their left, its bushy tail, twitching in annoyance.

"Oh, that's Agatha, by the way, don't mind her."

"She nearly scared me to death!" Chloe replied, calming herself.

A rainbow coloured parrot suddenly floated down the stairs, glided once around the room, then flew straight into the open cage, before turning and sitting on its perch.

"And that's Dorothy," he said with a lopsided smile.

"Well!" Percival asked. "What I have told you is true, however far-fetched it may seem. Now, please, tell what has happened, from the very beginning."

Sam recounted her story, with the other two butting in occasionally to add their own take on it and especially their uncomfortable confrontation with the other Sol Constantine. She handed him the diary and he looked at its cover before placing it on a nearby table.

The Percival figure, that said it was Mr Constantine, had now taken on an ashen complexion, but did not interrupt once. When the girls had finished, he sighed, his lips drawn tight then turned his back on them and took a few steps towards the window. Peering out the small square paned window, he began to speak.

"What I am about to tell you now will change your lives forever.

I will not even bother with the obvious question to ask you to leave and forget about what has transpired. It is too late for that ... You are here, that is enough," he sighed, straightened his back and turned to face the girls. With one hand, he reached up and picked the glasses off the end of his nose. "It's funny," he almost said to himself. "I don't need these when I am in Percival's body, yet I still wear them."

'Mr Constantine ... Percival!' Sam thought he looked somewhat distracted and almost jittery, muddled somehow, as if he was carrying the weight of the world on his shoulders. "Oh, sorry ... Yes, OK, where do I start?" Come on, Sol, pull yourself together. You're still their teacher remember. OK, here goes. "The name you know me by, Sol Constantine, is correct. However, I am also a Guardian of the Earth." He held his hand up to stop the girls before they started asking questions. "Let me finish, please and all will be revealed," he said in the manner that Mr Constantine would use, with his normal whimsical charm.

He was already beginning to 'pull himself together', thought Sam. "Percival Lamberts" he said, pointing to himself, which made him look pretty stupid in Sam's eyes, "is also a Guardian of the Earth. You mentioned the story he told you around the camp fire before he disappeared, about the creatures being banished beneath the earth, yes."

They nodded in silent unison, as if transfixed by a bright light.

"Well, that was all true."

"What!" blurted out Jazz in disbelief. "No way!"

"I assure you, my dear, it is. We, the Guardians are here to protect the Earth, to make sure that they never get out, never escape, because if they did, the world as we know it would end. No amounts of weapons or bombs could stop the things that are entombed beneath the land."

"But that happened thousands of years ago?" Chloe asked, saying what Sam was thinking. "So how come you know all this?"

"That's because we were there," he paused, making sure that they had heard correctly. "We are immortal. We were chosen as keepers, at the time of incarceration, as we were the ones who helped defeat and imprison the lizard race. They are called the Skree, and they have been mankind's foes for all time. We were entrusted by the people of that time and bestowed with the magic of the ages to make us immortal, to watch over the prison, to make sure that the magic that keeps them entombed is retained for all eternity. We have lived through the ages of man, never interfering, watching, staying hidden, caring for the moor and the prison beneath."

"So, you are prison guards then?" Chloe said nonchalantly, in her practical way as if this whole story was just an everyday event.

Percival grimaced. "You could say that. Now it seems that something is greatly amiss." Percival knew, that's why he was in my body in the week on the moor to check the stones," he said pointing to the journal. "He wanted a younger stronger body, just in case, but it wasn't enough. He knew, he told me and I didn't believe him. He knew. You know, it doesn't matter how old you are, you can still make mistakes. Time can make you complacent. And we could all pay. We have to free him. He is the one with the knowledge, the power to put this right. We just have to rescue him, that's all, no problem." Again, he was almost talking to himself, oblivious of the company about him.

"We're coming with you. Right, ladies?" Sam said before she knew it. "Wherever that might be!" she added. "Oh, we forgot to tell you about the stone crosses," she suddenly remembered. All three of them had forgotten!

"What about the stone crosses?"

"They have been vandalised, knocked down, it's disgraceful," Jazz spoke out. The other two looked at her with a sideways glance of disbelief.

"Oh no, this is getting worse, minute by minute. We must not waste any time. We must find, and free, Percival now. He will know what to do ... I hope."

"You hope?" Sam asked.

"Well, yes, he should know what to do; he imprisoned them there in the first place. Now come, we must make haste."

He pulled on a big long overcoat from off a hook behind the door and swung it open, but suddenly paused, looking back at the room briefly, then directly at Sam. "Dorothy needs feeding twice a day and Agatha takes care of herself, but likes company, though." he said a little sadly.

He seemed to be speaking to Sam, but she noticed his lips didn't move, and the others did not seem to have heard! "What ...?" she started to say, but he pushed them out the house, leading the girls to a rusty beaten up old green Range Rover parked in the drive, to the left of the house. He reached the car and stopped, raising both hands out, just above the level of the bonnet. He stood for a moment, dead still, his back to the girls.

"Mr ... Constantine. Are you OK?" asked a bemused Chloe.

"Yes, fine thanks, I was just instilling the car with the speed of a thousand Elven Horses and the heart of a British Lion."

"They had lions in Britain." Chloe exclaimed, goofily.

"Actually, I was thinking of the rugby team, but yes, we did, once. Wonderful grand beasts, as large as a cow and as white as the snow. True Kings of the Animal World. Oh, those were the days."

"Elven Horses?" Sam inquired.

"Fastest horses on the planet. Could outrun the wind, you know. And sometimes they would have to, if you came across any Trolls!"

The more Sam looked at Percival/Mr Constantine, the more she realised, she hardly recognised him, them. Whether it was due to the change of minds, she was not sure, but she felt that she would soon find out.

"Is this some sort of magic car?" she asked shyly, her words sounding completely stupid. "A magic car! What's this? Back to the Future 4!" Jazz smirked sarcastically in disbelief.

"Of course it's not a magic car, it's just a normal Range Rover, I've just instilled it with some magic, just in case!"

"Oh brother!" Jazz added. "Somebody take me home. Everyone's gone crazy!"

Sam looked at the old man. "Just ignore her, she'll come round, you know what she is like."

CHAPTER 5 - MAGIC!

Half an hour later, they stood atop the moor, looking back over Cadover Bridge and the clay pits beyond. They had bundled the bikes into the back of Percival's green Range Rover and then headed up onto the moor. Slowing down as they had come to the first fallen cross, Percival shook his head, his face a picture of utter disbelief.

Parking near to where they had camped only two nights ago, they stood in stunned silence for a few moment's contemplation as they looked upon the second fallen cross, before hiking up the hill to a small littering of boulders scattered about a cairn of stones. One stone boulder stood upright, set into the earth. In the middle of the stone, a large oval hole had been cut into it, sometime in the distant past, which made it now look almost as if it had been formed this way. Sam suddenly recognised the scene from the picture atop the fireplace in the Old Toll House.

"You will each have to climb through the hole in the stone and then walk around it anti-clockwise nine times!" said Percival with a wry smile.

"You're kidding, right!" replied Jazz, looking in disgust at the dirty hole in the stone.

"No, not at all. If you want to stay here, fine, but if you want to help me get my body back and save Percival as well?" he said "Then, this is the only way to enter the realm beneath the Earth." Wind ruffled his tuft of wispy grey hair, giving it a life all of its own. He had one hand resting on the stone above the hole, and his head was turned to the group, his deep-set eyes, twinkled with mysterious knowledge.

"Just follow me, oh ... And don't look back."

"DON'T LOOK BACK!" all three girls replied in sync.

"Why not?" Sam questioned, suspiciously.

"Best not to know, really," he replied a little too quickly, as a hint of nervousness coursed through his voice.

"Oh, well that makes it better!" Chloe retorted with a large hint of sarcasm.

The old man rose, standing upright, facing towards the girls, one hand still upon the stone. "Let me put this as clearly as I can. The earth is in peril, the person we need to help us has been captured by the bad guys! We are the only hope to save him and prevent the end of life as we know it. Every moment, we stand here, we are wasting time! Now are you coming or not?"

"Well, if you put it like that." Chloe replied, with a stupid grin, arms outstretched.

"Shut up, Chloe!" Sam and Jazz shouted in unison.

"OK, we're coming," Sam answered, thinking that perhaps this was all a dream, that she had actually bumped her head far worse than she thought and she was really still in the land of the fairies. In a minute she would wake up and see her mum's concerned face looking down on her. But even as she thought this, somehow, she knew that this was just too real. And as if to test her faith, it started to rain, a light summer drizzle that would not last long because there was very little cloud, but raining it was, and she could feel the cold drops hitting her head and shoulders. Everything felt so real, too real to be a dream, she thought again.

Without another word, Percival knelt and lowered himself level with the hole and proceeded to climb through. Sam clambered through, then started following the old man anti-clockwise around the stone, her eyes firmly fixed onto Percival's back. She instinctively felt a presence behind her, but hesitated, just as she was about to peer over her shoulder, the warning, 'Don't look back!' rang in her ears. With supreme willpower, she refocused on Percival and started counting down the circles in her mind.

Jazz was the last through, with a few quips about getting her clothes dirty, she saw Chloe looking at her as she exited the other side. She widened her eyes and made a close-lipped plea, and understanding Chloe quickly snapped her head around and rejoined the imaginary line behind Sam. Rain was still falling as, a few minutes later, they all stopped and shuffled in close together beside Percival.

"Good, now, Sam, you stand here, please," he said dragging her by the shoulders to a piece of earth that looked just like any other piece of earth upon the moor. "Jazz here," he said pointing to a spot behind and to the left of Sam. "And finally, Chloe here," he said again, pointing to another spot behind and to the right of Sam this time. The girls looked at each other, eyes raised, an internal head shake, forming.

"I think that's right!" he almost said to himself. "Oh well, here goes."

Sam's hair was beginning to get wet now, tiny rivulets of cold rainwater were dripping down her neck, sending a shiver down her spine and as she reached up to wipe them off, she lost her footing a touch and took a step to her left.

"Sam!" the old man's voice came again. "Just take one step to your right please."

"Oh, for goodness sake ... OK ... but why?" Sam retorted, moving back to her old position. He had turned to face them now, legs apart, arms outstretched and palms to the sky. "You'll see," he replied whimsically, and then closed his eyes and spoke a sentence in a tongue that none of the girls had ever heard before, in a language that sounded older than time itself. Suddenly, a feeling of rushing air was preceded by a moment's utter silence and for the briefest of heartbeats it felt as if the earth and everything upon it had stopped dead in its tracks, frozen in time. And then the sounds of the world returned. Sam, who had been holding her breath without even knowing, let out a deep sigh and then jumped with fright, when she turned her head to see a large stone column literally within arm's reach of her. She turned slowly, utter amazement covering the expression on her face as she looked wide eyed at the ruins of a large circular building scattered about them. Giant columns of stone stretched into the heights, maybe 40 feet high, blotting out the sky, where moments before, they had stood beside a cairn and a stone with a hole in it! "Jazz! Chloe!" she called, looking about her.

"Over here, we're OK," Chloe called back from behind a stone outcrop.

"How ...? How did you do that? Have we moved, been transported somewhere?" But even as she asked, she could see that the landscape in the foreground hadn't changed. She could still see Cadover, the hills to the north and the clay pits.

"No, we haven't moved, but you can see why I had to move you, though," Percival said, bushy eyebrows lifted "Didn't want you to end up with a few tons of stone on top of you, did I?"

"Gee, thanks!" Sam replied, somewhat sarcastically. By now the other two had joined her, their mouths agape. "How have you done this? Where are we?" Sam suddenly realised that it had stopped raining, but her eyes narrowed as she looked about her and saw that she could still see the rain, but somehow, it wasn't reaching them! She walked forward to the end of the ruins, past the last fallen stone and saw now, very clearly, a line on the earth, where the rain was falling and dampening the ground, but everything within the line was dry. It just wasn't reaching the earth, it seemed to be disappearing in mid-air!

She reached out in bewilderment, her hand slowly moving towards what she thought must be some sort of protective shield. As she raised her head, she could almost make out, even imagine, a giant bubble covering their position, which nothing could penetrate.

"This is amazing!" she said quietly, peering further afield, beyond the invisible boundary and to Sam, everything else looked the same. "What has happened?" she said, putting her hand to where she thought the barrier was. Sam felt nothing, nothing solid, no give, just the tingle of cold rain on her fingertips as she stretched her hand further outside the invisible field. Sam turned her palm to the sky and cupped it to catch some rainwater, feeling the water gathering in her hand, then retracted her arm. As she drew it inside the shield, the rainwater was gone, her hand dry! She looked up at Percival as he approached, her eyes questioning.

"That is the magic ... of magic," he replied simply, smiling widely. He raised his head and peered about him at the ruins. "No one can see us or hear us from outside. No one can get in unless they know how and there are only two other men who know how, and one is already here! This is always here, hidden to the outside world. This," he said pointing to the invisible bubble, "is a distraction shield. We haven't moved. I have just opened your eyes. The distraction shield works like a magician. A good magician works on sleight of hand, making your eyes and mind think one thing is happening, while in fact, in the other hand, just the opposite could be taking place. This is how this works. It stops man, beast and even the elements themselves from breaking through. Anyone or anything that approaches here now, will only see the cairn and holed out stone. If they come near it, they are subconsciously nudged away. We have entered into a different time phase if it is easier to understand. That is the magic of it. Follow me," he said to the three girls and strode off around a column.

"You see, here is the stone with the hole in it ..." And then he stopped, his whole frame going as taught as a piano wire. "Oh no!" he exclaimed, looking down at the stone, then whipping his head back to face the three, his eyes wide in fear and anger.

"Who looked back?" he whispered through gritted teeth. He rose above them, suddenly looking scary and frightened, all in one. Stunned silence held sway for a moment, at the quick change in mood. "Quickly, who looked back? Quickly?" he said again more urgently as he reached into his coat for something.

And then it was upon them. And what came at them was something out of a children's fantasy book nightmare. Launching itself from atop the nearest column was a creature with a body of black fur and long spindly, hairy legs. Its giant, insect like, black eyes locked onto Chloe and never wavered off its target. It was a huge spider, thought Sam at first in her slow-motion state of shock, but somehow worse, somehow more frightening as it had an almost sinister human appearance about it. The thing landed on Jazz, pushing her down and pinning her to the floor while knocking Sam aside with one of its long front legs, its glistening black eyes still firmly fixed on Chloe. For a moment, it just sat atop Jazz, who was too stunned to even shout or try and move, then with a tense of its eight powerful legs it sprang forward towards a transfixed Chloe, mandibles open and clicking in anticipation.

And then, in a blur of speed, Percival was there, standing between the thing and the girl, a silver crucifix held out before him. Another short incantation and the horrifying creature was halted in mid-flight, as if it had hit a wall.

Sam watched as a high-pitched whining escaped from the monstrosity. Its legs constricted inwards and with its forward momentum paused, it fell like a stone to the earth, before righting itself and scuttling off into the ruins.

"What the hell was that?" Sam almost shouted, leaning against one of the columns for support.

Percival was still standing statuesque in front of Chloe, still holding the crucifix aloft. Behind him, Chloe was holding her hands to her ears, curled up with her knees pulled in, eyes wide in fright. "Wow!" he said looking at the crucifix in admiration. "Never done that before." he said almost cheerfully. "Didn't even know if it would work?" he spoke again to himself as a proud afterthought, but Sam could see the strain in the Percival's eyes and the way he faltered when he straightened up.

"Mr Constantine/Percival!" Sam shouted.

"Oh sorry, I'm sure Percival has probably done that before but I haven't," he said excitedly, and then saw the sternness on the girls faces and refrained from smiling instantly. "Sorry," he stammered.

"I'm covered in goo!" Jazz spoke in disgust, trying to unstick herself from the silky residue that the spider thing had left on her. "I don't believe it, this is a new top!"

Sam was beginning to think she was the only one that thought being attacked by a giant spider thing was out of the ordinary. She raised her eyes and shook her head, and started laughing at the stupidity of the response.

"Jazz, I think we have more important things to worry about!" as she turned back to Percival. "What are you, a vampire hunter now?"

Percival looked quizzically at the silver cross in his hand then back to Sam. "In this instance, it is the silver they fear not the cross. The silver has certain properties that weaken them ... like ... "

"Like Kryptonite to Superman," Chloe's voice came from behind them as she got to her feet.
"You looked back didn't you?"
"Yes, but only for ... "
"It doesn't matter, you have released your shadowchaser now."
A foreboding sense of dread crept through Sam's mind as she looked at the downcast and scared Chloe. Instinctively, she reached out and put her arms around her friend's shoulder, giving her a big hug, noticing tears of fear in eyes. Gritting her teeth, she turned back to the old man. "So, what's a shadowchaser when it is at home? And why did you say, 'your shadowchaser', to Chloe?"
Percival took a deep breath and swallowed before continuing, his eyes averting from the girls. "It's a creature born from your shadow. As soon as you looked back, just for that instant, it was formed by the black magic that is created when a spell is reversed or broken. From now on, wherever you cast a big enough shadow of yourself, the shadowchaser will be freed to come for you. It will never give up, it does not tire and you cannot kill it, you cannot stop it, only silver can keep it at bay."
"What does it want?" Chloe said through shaking teeth.
"We think it wants to take over your body, but we are not sure really, it has not happened for some time and the book's we consult are not always easy to understand! It wants to take you over and control you, to become you ... " He handed her the cross. The cross had a thin piece of black leather attached to it that was long enough to put around her neck. "Here, take this and never let it leave your sight from now on. Never, for even the slightest moment. With that you will be safe ... ish. I'm sorry ... "
"Sorry ... sorry ... oh, that makes it better, then," Chloe said crying.
"I hate spiders anyway even when they are tiny and this one's the size of a man!" she said with a grim smile. "Don't worry, Chloe, we will find a way, we are in it together, remember," Sam said, hug-

ging her again. Jazz just nodded, tongue tied for once.

"There must be a way to stop the thing, right, Percival?" she questioned towards Percival, and suddenly realised she was calling him Percival again. 'It didn't feel right to call him

Mr Constantine! It wouldn't be Mr Constantine until he looked like Mr Constantine.' she decided.

"There might be, but I know of none. But Percival might if we can get him back in here," he said tapping his head. "He is your only hope. His knowledge is far far greater than mine, which he reminds me of constantly, by the way. Come, the creature is licking its wounds for now, we need to find my body and get Percival's mind back where it belongs, so come on, time is even more precious now."

He led them at a quick stride to the hole in the stone, and they were amazed to see behind the stone, a sunken dry well. On closer inspection, a flight of small circular steps wound its way down into the impenetrable darkness.

"No way am I going down there!" Jazz exclaimed. "That's looks even dirtier than the hole in the stone."

The other two girls just looked at each other and shook their heads.

"Just ignore our friend, she doesn't like getting her hands dirty, do you, hon?" Sam said in a sarcastic but jokey manner. The cheeks on Jazz's face started to redden, but Percival ignored the banter and spoke up.

"This is the entrance to the world beneath the Earth, where the enemies of man have been cast. Much danger lies before us on this path, but this is the only way we can enter this realm and find my friend, so please do not hesitate."

"You know with tactful words like that, you could win anyone over, you'd make a great teacher!" Chloe retorted.

"I am a teacher!" Percival replied, rolling his eyes. "Remember!"

"Oops, forgot about that!" Chloe replied with a lopsided smile and gap toothy grin.

CHAPTER 6 - INTO DARKNESS!

Sam looked at the hole and took an involuntary gulp and step back. All she could see was the impenetrable darkness below her, beckoning her, enticing her to see what lay beyond what her eyes could not see. A line of stone stairs spiralled downwards around the outer wall, disappearing some 20 steps below into the shadows. For an instance, she wondered if they actually continued and if so, for how long? The steps looked almost new. She expected them to be worn, sculpted by the countless tread of many feet through the ages of man. But then she realised that below them was a prison of sorts, but this one was beneath the earth, hidden from mankind for countless centuries. The stairs looked new because they had not been used. They had been constructed at the time as an access to the world below and then left for eons, untouched by human feet, until now! Yet somehow, after all this time, the inmates had found a way out of the asylum and the world was again in peril.

Percival led the way. "Keep close to the wall on your left as you go down," he said, stating the obvious. "Wouldn't want you falling into the … Oops … Done it again, haven't I? Sorry!" as he looked back at their nervous faces.

They started off, Sam following Percival, again. The steps were just wide enough for one person to stand on them at a time, and Sam thought it would be hard to change positions, if it had to be done. As soon as they were beneath the level of the well, Sam felt the immediate drop in temperature. She shivered, feeling goose bumps spreading across her exposed skin. Only the echoing sound of their footsteps and the scraping of clothes on rock eclipsed the total beckoning darkness. Percival was moving steadily on at a reasonable, assured, pace leaving the ever-decreasing light above them without a backward glance. She noticed that despite the age of Percival, the old man moved with the grace and dexterity of a young man and she wondered if this was due to the young mind in the old body or perhaps, he was just more supple than he actually looked.

Sam looked up and a thought skittered through her already tired mind, 'I hope I see the light of day again.'

As if in response, a click in front of her made her start and suddenly, for a few paces below and above them, the well erupted with the neon light of a torch. Water dripped from moss covered stone to disappear into the depths. Creatures scurried away into darkened recesses afraid of the light.

"Didn't think I'd come without one, now, did you?" Percival peered back with a Cheshire cats grin.

'I don't believe this!' Sam thought, shaking her head at the absurdity of it all. 'We are following a strange old madman into a dark hole in the ground. And I don't know who is more mad, me for following you or you for doing it!' she wanted to say, but thought that perhaps now was not the right time.

Percival pointed the light back up the tunnel. "Everyone OK?" he said. No one spoke, the girls just nodded. "Then let's keep going." The light at the top was nearly gone altogether. All that remained was a tiny dwindling circle of light and for the first time, Sam felt the weight of the countless tons of earth pushing down on her from above. The well seemed to narrow as the light above them became a mere pinprick. It almost looked as if the well itself was folding in upon itself as they descended further and further, into the depths of the Earth. Like a dark creature of the void, claustrophobia gripped her in its claws and squeezed the air from her lungs. She suddenly stumbled on a loose rock that skidded off the side into the pitch blackness. She tensed waiting for the sound of its landing, but silence prevailed.

"My God, how deep does this go?" she exclaimed in horror, feeling the expanse of nothingness to her right. Instinctively she leant against the wall, feeling the stairs shrinking in her mind's eye, and waiting for the shadowy hand of darkness to grasp her and pull her down screaming into the depths below.

"We are here," Percival said, pointing his torch into the wall on his left. Sam noticed the stairs had levelled off onto a ledge and a small alcove was set into the rock. An arch led into a further chamber beyond, which seemed lit by some unearthly light emanating from the entrance itself. A green shimmering beam, made up of thousands of pinpricks of light covered the arch and rock. Chloe and Jazz bundled onto the ledge with a deep sigh of relief.

"This is the entrance to the world below. When we have crossed this, they will sense us in their domain. You must be prepared to run and fight if necessary. Run being the operative option," he said raising his eyebrows.

"And if we can't run?" Jazz asked.

"Then we fight ... not with our hands, but our mouths?"

"What! So, you want me to tell them a story, then? That should do it!" Sam said sardonically, in nervous excitement.

"Not quite, but if anyone can talk them to death, you can," he said under his breath.

"I heard that."

"Now listen, just remember these words. Look them in the eyes and say, 'Solumne lumme extracto.' Got it. 'Solumne lumme extracto.' And if that doesn't work, well just run, oh, and remember, don't look back!"

"Why not this time?" Chloe retorted in desperation.

"Nothing much, you just might fall over a stone or something. You should always look where you are running. It's common sense."

"Rrrr, if those things don't kill you, I might just do them a favour. You're unreal." Sam replied, shaking her head again, but smiling at the old man before them. She had never before been so outspoken and forward towards an adult, especially her supply teacher, but somehow, this man and this situation, had brought about this change of approach.

"Oh no!" Percival said, looking down at the torch, which was flickering and already beginning to turn a dim yellow. "I forgot to replace the batteries!"

Shaking her head again, Sam ignored the comment, feeling that time was drifting away like sand through her fingers.

"The way seems lit," she said pointing through the arch. "Do you have any idea where

Mr Constantine could be? Are we going on a wild goose chase or do you have an idea you haven't told us?"

"Not yet, No and Yes!" he said smiling stupidly after a few seconds thought, holding aloft one forefinger.

"You know, if I had a younger sister, she could never be more annoying than you! Talk English! Female 13-year-old English, if you can!"

"OK, what I haven't told you is that I should be able to go straight to Mr Constantine, my body, once we are inside the underworld. That barrier is shielding our link. As soon as I step through, I should know where he is. The only thing is, they will know we are coming."

"How do you know he is still alive?" Chloe asked.

"Because if he feels pain, then so do I! Anyway, they might have caught him, but killing him is a different matter. Guardians are immortal. They can't kill him, they can only imprison him ... us."

Some thought drifted through the teacher's mind. For the first time since leaving his house, Percival's normal calm appearance wavered. Doubt circled his eyes and he pursed his lips for just the briefest of moments, and then it was gone. He locked eyes on the group, his face set in a grim but stern and determined look.

"Time to play," he smiled and took something out of his pocket and without a backward glance, slung it into the well. They heard the tinkling of things as they bounced off the walls before descending into the darkness.

"What was that?" Chloe asked, eyebrows raised.

"Old rusty iron nails. They hate iron. Drives them crazy at the thought of it. Remember that. Now come on, that should have bought us some time," he turned and stepped through the veil and continued through. The others followed and somewhere in the distant depths they heard a deep bellowing roar that sent shivers down their spines and fear in their minds. The race was on.

CHAPTER 7 - THE RESCUE

From the entrance chamber, they followed a solitary unwelcoming tunnel that snaked its way deeper into the earth. A moss looking lichen, that clung to the ceilings gave off an eerie luminance that they were somewhat thankful for. The walls were painted with amazing murals, depicting countless scenes of battles. Fire breathing Dragons and giant ogre like creatures came to life in the moss light, and the numerous lizard creatures with their snake-like eyes gave Sam the feeling that they were watching her, urging her on into their domain. The temperature had dropped even lower and a coldness hung in the air causing their breaths to form in front of them as they traversed the spiralling corridor, ever downwards, in stunned silence. Even breathing seemed to be an effort. Suddenly the corridor started to level off and they exited it into a huge cavern with row upon row of giant stone columns, each 20 foot in diameter, disappearing into the heights above them. The distant ceiling above, and the far walls to their sides, were not visible but they sensed, rather than saw, the enormity of the cavern. Every step on the stone floor echoed around the chamber, resonating in the Cathedral like cavern. Lichen clung to only some of the stones, almost as if to point out the direction they should take.

"It's this way," Percival's spoke quietly, pointing straight down the line of the nearest columns. "He is close now," He moved them on, never letting them stop to think about things.

As they passed beneath the columns, Sam looked up in awe at the sights. They reminded her of the Temple of Luxor, in Egypt, which she had studied about recently, but these seemed even bigger and the drawings seemed to predate even that ancient civilisation. 'How old was this place?' She thought.

They reached an arched doorway and entered to see a row of dungeons on their left. Iron grates, that were set into the rock itself, stretched along one side for as far as they could see. Each section was divided by more grates, disappearing into the gloom of a large cave. Percival led them on, past dungeons that held ghoulish contents, skeletons hanging from chains and the threadbare rags of clothing, marking the last resting place of someone who had perished down here. They neared a rock face with a wooden door set into it, and in the last dungeon before this, Percival turned, spoke a sentence in some strange tongue and the gate swung open with a loud grating of iron on iron.

They saw movement in the darkness and then Mr Constantine appeared, his mouth gagged by a black cloth. Percival immediately ripped the cloth off and they both clasped hands, relief showing on their faces to see each other again.

"About time!" Percival said. "I've been here for quite some time! I was nearly giving up hope, you know. But that is the wonderful thing about humans that makes them different from every other species on this planet, they have the attribute of hope, and hope is something that is born within every human that drives them on, even in the darkest of times, when all seems lost. You know ... "

"I know you have been on your own for a few days, but that is enough of the speeches, old man," Mr Constantine said with a wry smile and raise of his eyes, knowing that Percival had a history of rambling on.

'A few days!' Sam thought. And then it dawned on her. "You've swapped back?" she asked. "Just like that? No Vulcan mind meld stuff?"

"No" they both said in union, and even Jazz nearly smiled.

"And why are you three here?" the true Percival asked of the girls.

"The last I saw you girls, was on your trip," pointing at Sam. "And it was you I saw just before I was captured. They tried to get you too."

Sam nodded, shivering at the memory of how it all started.

"This is no place for children," Percival said harshly to the younger man. Mr Constantine quickly whispered something to him, then he added, "Oh," was all he said at first, looking bemused. "It looks like I owe you a debt of gratitude," he said bowing as if saluting royalty.

"A knight to the end, Percival," Mr Constantine said which Sam found amusing. 'Wasn't Percival one of the Knights of the Round Table?' she asked herself.

"Let's get out of here while we can," he said to Percival.

"Agreed, but I need to check the sword, to see if it is still intact and the magic is strong. The stones are moving, the Dragon is restless. It means Moribund is up to something. I gave up believing in coincidences 500 years ago."

"OK, but we need to do it quickly, these tunnels are going to be swarming in minutes!" They walked to the door, opened it and walked through, the girls close behind.

"Oh no!" Percival exclaimed. The room was not huge, nor empty, but held a large dais in its the middle. Tunnels led off this main antechamber, in considerable numbers. Upon the dais lay the figure of a knight, bathed in a beautiful clear blue light. The face was godlike, chiselled from a statue. Blond curls showed beneath an iron helmet and he lay on his back, over six feet in length, arms crossed, with the hilt of a sword resting upon his chest. The figure was dressed in what looked like white linen, showing off the huge frame beneath. A man or something that resembled a man, stood upon the dais, a look of puzzlement spreading across his face. He stood like a headmaster at assembly looking down on his school, body erect, hands behind his back. The man looked like Sol Constantine, but Sam knew it wasn't. This was? What did they call him? 'Moribund.' she remembered. Behind and to the side of the man crouched countless Skree, their eyes twinkling in the dark, like stars in the night sky. They stood erect on two feet, but bent over, arms hanging in front of them, awaiting an order, a soft murmuring coming from their strange shaped mouths. The darkness showed little other features to the stunned girls, but the quiet noise they made was unearthly and scary.

"Ah, just in time," a voice chortled. "Well well, what have we here? If it isn't the sorcerer and his apprentice. And, oh look, he has brought some new recruits too," Moribund spread his left arm theatrically to encompass the girls. "Not quite the Knights of the Round Table are they, ... Merlin?" The girls turned their heads in unison to stare at Mr Constantine, jaws agape, eyes wide.

"Merlin?" Jazz said in stunned amazement.

"They will do," Sol Constantine replied sternly.

"Merlin?" Sam said in shock looking at her teacher as if he had grown another head. "You said that he had all the knowledge to help."

"He has," Sol winked. "And Merlin was a long time ago. I'm Sol Constantine now," he turned to face his lookalike. "You can't touch the sword, Moribund, it will burn you, so forget it, let us leave peacefully, or ... "

"Or what? You see, Merlin, you've lost your touch. Capturing you, Percival, whatever, was a bonus. I just wanted to get out, not to escape, but to get something!"

"What something?" Percival asked with apprehension.

"These," Moribund said smiling, bringing his hands into view, with a large pair of gloves on. "Heavy duty fire retardant gloves. £19.99 from the local store. Oh, isn't the 21st century wonderful. I don't know why I didn't think of it sooner."

Sol's face had gone white, drained of colour. For the briefest of moments, his eyes now looked like that of a frightened rabbit, and his lips had drawn back into a grimace of resolute fear. And then it was gone, his inner demons banished, his composure recaptured. He took a deep breath, his face taking on a look of grim determination. "It will still burn you, you know that. Don't be a fool."

"Fool, hah. Easy for you to say. I've waited centuries for this moment. The Morn stones have fallen, the Dragons bones are coming free and the barrier between your world and mine is disintegrating before your very eyes. Soon all of us will be set free. And then we can walk the earth again and reign in our rightful place where we belong. You and your friend have hunted us and destroyed everyone of us that escapes, one by one, while we were trapped down here watching all the suffering you have heaped on our race. Your hands are tainted with our blood forever. And you know, when we are free, I will imprison you down here for all eternity, with the knowledge that you have failed the whole human race. I know I cannot kill you, but I will bury you so deep, you will never be able to free yourselves. Anyway, what gives your race any more right to live on top of the Earth than us, while we are banished beneath it, to live in the shadows, waiting and suffering in the dank bowels beneath your feet, eh?"

"We have the right because we wanted to live in peace, while you just wanted to destroy everything that was good about humanity. You wanted to wipe us off the face of the planet."

"To purify the Earth and start afresh with our race only, that is all. I see nothing wrong with that! It matters not, now that I have the hilt of Excalibur, nothing can stop me. Mankind will be no more. It is already too late. The Dragon will rise tonight and nothing you can do can stop me."

With that, Moribund reached down and without hesitation, picked up the hilt of the sword. The sword hilt looked old and dirty, and a piece of leather that was part of the handle had frayed and was hanging loose. The blade was broken in a jagged V-shape about two inches from the hilt. In the light emanating from the figure below him upon the dais, they could all see Moribund grimace, but his smug smile of satisfaction and raised eyes towards the group, showed his exaltation. As he raised the hilt in front of him, so the figure on the dais started to change, the features started to contort and shrivel as if being burnt. The light started to dim and in just a few seconds the figure's clothes, skin and internal organs had disintegrated, leaving a skeleton upon the dais. It had all happened so fast, no one had even moved. "There, it is done. The prison is no longer."

"No, Arthur!" Sol said forlornly, and then with an angry shout he squared up, peering at Moribund. "And what then, when you have killed the last human, destroyed all the birds and beasts? What then? You'll stop the fighting, put down your weapons and live happily ever after in peace! I think not. You know nothing but murder, death, carnage and mayhem. You'll start squabbling amongst yourselves, factions will form, new enemies created and then you will destroy each other, so that in the end, no one will remain. You know no other way. That is why we fight you, to protect life in all forms."

Sol had been steadily moving towards the dais, but on a gradual angle so that any moment, he would cross in front of Percival. Sam somehow knew instinctively that this had been rehearsed. She saw out the corner of her eye as Percival nonchalantly put his hands in his pockets.

"So, how did you get out Moribund? It couldn't have been easy?" Sol asked.

"Very good," Moribund said slowly, twitching his forefinger at the group. "Stalling for time so that you can think of a way to stop me. I think not. Last time you stopped me you had Arthur and the Knights, now you have three children ... " he said wide eyed in mock fear. "and now Arthur sleeps the eternal sleep. He won't be riding to your rescue this time. And they are just young girls." he added, laughing at the absurdity of it.

"Hey!" said Chloe. "What's your problem with girls?"

'Good girl, Chloe. Keep it up' thought Sam. Moribund just shook his head and looked at the hilt of the sword for a moment. He constantly swapped it between hands as if by doing so, the pain he was feeling would be less, almost as if he was juggling a cactus, she thought.

"How did you get out?" Sol asked again.

"Do you know how many of my brethren have died, so I could escape. No, you wouldn't have a clue. We have waited and watched you. Plotted and planned. We know what you have been up to, Merlin, you and your friends. For centuries we have been looking for a weakness in the shield that holds us trapped, a fissure through which we could escape. You see, ladies," he said turning to face the girls. "If we but touch the prisons outer defences, we will burn and keep burning until we die." He snapped his head back to the two adults. "I can sense when you are near, Merlin, we watched as you walked the moors, taking notes in your precious little book. You knew we were up to something, didn't you? And when you stood on one of the Dragons teeth, a tear in the fissure appeared, tiny at first. Oh yes, your power somehow caused it. How ironic, that by your hand you entombed us and by your hand you will free us. One after another I forced my brethren through the tiny hole, each one screaming in agony as they perished. But with each one's sacrifice, so the gap increased, until I could squeeze between the terrified dying creatures, reach out and grasp you. Oh, you should have seen you face, it was quite something."

"I'm sure it was," Sol said. "But it wasn't me, was it? That must have annoyed you, almost as much as this ..." and with that he ducked, while at the same time, Percival slung something towards the dais, something that looked to Sam like a normal plain wax candle. Almost at the same time, Sol flung a load of old coins in a slow arc that scattered the lizard people backwards into the shadows. The candle struck the stone dais and caused an amazing effect. She heard Percival mumbling something just before it struck and then suddenly, a green light shot out in all directions. Moribund screamed, a horrible bestial scream of pain and anguish, all in one. The hilt dropped from his left hand, clanged once on the front of the dais before dropping off the edge to be caught by the outstretched hands of Sol, who juggled it a couple of times before grasping it with both hands.

"Run!" he shouted and turned, shepherding the girls in front of him. "Back the same way, and don't stop until we reach the top."

Moribund's face contorted in anguish, his rage palpable beneath his semi translucent skin. Black tendrils started to erupt from different parts of his body, straining towards the group, the tentacles twitching and changing direction as they tried to sense their prey. "After them!" he screeched to the confused and frightened Skree.

Percival was first through the doorway into the dungeon area, pausing to hurry the girls on. The doorway was small and the pathway past the dungeon bars was only just wide enough for two. Sol literally burst through the doorway last, stumbling and being righted at the last moment by the welcome outstretched hand of Percival. The girls had momentarily stopped.

"Run, keep going until you reach the top!" they shouted again in unison.

A horde of black pulsing bodies literally swarmed through the opening, and to their horror, some scrambled up the wall above the entrance as nimble as spiders, disappearing into the shadows above. Some swung from bar to bar like monkeys, closing in on the group in seconds. Others slid forward on hands and knees, dragging their arms behind them. A screeching, chattering and slapping of body on rock as they moved along the walls to their left and right, resounded around the empty walls giving Sam the horrible feeling that they were being outflanked. Thousands of pinpricks of light flickered en masse to either side of them, like embers in the wind. She heard Percival shout something over the din, making the closest Skree recoil back in horror as if they had been struck by some physical and tangible force. They entered the Cathedral chamber at a breathless run. The group was stretched out now, with Sam at the front and Sol the last. The noise now had become deafening, echoing off the distant walls and reverberating back twice as loud. Not only were their own footsteps upon the stone floor loud, but the creatures that followed screeched and squealed as if it was feeding time for the monkeys, at a zoo. Even as they ran, so a heaving mass of primeval horror closed in on them like the dark attacking a dying candle. Ahead of Sam, the entrance leading to the well appeared, but just as her hopes rose, a fast-moving line of lizard people appeared from behind the columns to either side, joining up seamlessly to encircle the group and cut off their line of retreat. 'We are trapped!' Sam thought in panic.

"Keep going," Percival shouted beside her, while raising and throwing another candle all in one motion, followed by a few choice words. The closest Skree ducked and turned, just in time, to see it hit the stone floor behind. Another bright green light lit up the darkness and the Skree parted and scattered away, leaving the coast clear for Sam to race to the tunnel entrance. She stopped, catching her breath as Percival, Jazz and then Sol joined them. The Skree had stopped pursuing suddenly.

"Where's Chloe?" Sam asked, hands on knees, breathing heavily.

In shocked and stunned silence, they looked back into the seething mass of moving yellow eyes.

"Sam?" a weak voice came to them, from a short distance away, but somewhat muffled by the things between them.

"Chloe," she replied anxiously.

"I'm scared, Sam," she could hear the fear in her voice. Sol started forward but Percival pulled him back.

"Can't you do something?" Sam asked wide eyed in hope. The faint light from the lichen showed that the nearest Skree had their backs to them, almost as if they didn't exist anymore.

"I have no more Witches' Candles left!" Percival replied, he said reaching into his pockets. He brought out the torch and clicked it on, raising it high and pointing it towards where he thought Chloe's voice had come from. Barely 10 yards away, Chloe stood huddled on her own completely surrounded by lizard people. They were at least four-deep between her and the doorway. They stood staring at her in silence. Sam could see that she was shaking and clutching her arms around herself. And then something amazing happened. As the dim light from the torch hit Chloe, it cast a shadow across a small part of the floor and onto one of the Skree. Something burst out and through the Skree, killing it instantly. Something with eight legs, that moved like the wind, leapt over the stunned girl and attacked the nearest lizard that was blocking her path. It went down in seconds amid a flashing of arms and legs and the rest parted, screaming in fear, retreating into the darkness. Before anyone could move the spider thing, jumped back towards Chloe towering above her, peering intently into the shadows. It stood there like a sentinel, looming over her, not in an attacking way however but as her protector, daring anything to come at it.

"I don't believe it!" Sam heard Sol say. "I thought I'd seen it all, but … Chloe, come on," he beckoned. Chloe looked about her in bewilderment, first at the shadowchaser and then at the group.

She recoiled, scuttling back on her hands and elbows, but the shadowchaser followed her every move, keeping it between her and the amassing lizard people. Coming to her senses, she rose awkwardly and ran to them, embracing Sam with a sob.

"Come on, up the stairs, we will be safe when we get there. We are nearly there now," Sol said with a still somewhat amazed voice. The shadowchaser had back-pedalled to, nearly, where they were standing, its large black eyes, piercing the darkness for signs of movement.

"It's watching our backs!" Sam said in awe.

"Not ours, methinks ... hers." Percival said pointing at Chloe.

"We must move," Sol said ignoring the conversation. And move again they did. Keeping closer they hurried up the incline, passing the painted tunnel walls until they reached the gleaming entrance to the prison. Without hesitation, they passed through it and started to climb. When they had nearly reached the top, Sol paused and spoke in the ancient dialect, and when he finished, the stones beneath his feet began to retract into the wall, blocking the way up for the ones that would try to follow. Behind them in the tunnel the shadowchaser acted as a buffer until when the last was through the shield it simply dissolved into thin air, leaving the screaming and frustrated Skree to howl in derision. The first three crashed into the screen and dissolved in a flash of fire and the rest backed up chattering and screeching in annoyance that their prison was still very much intact, before turning and racing back down the tunnel.

CHAPTER 8 – TRAPPED

When Sam reached the top of the well, she flung herself over the side and lay there looking up into the sky, surprised to see that the sky was dark, the night upon them. She was breathing heavily after the hurried and frantic climb. She felt the others climbing out of the well and collapsing upon the earth around her. The evening sky had never looked so beautiful, so clear and bright with the light of the full moon. She took in a deep breath and let it out. It felt good to be back on top of the earth rather than beneath it.

"Oh no!" she heard Jazz say. "Er ...people?" she said to all of them. And they could sense the fear in her voice.

Weary limbs moved. Sam propped herself up on to one elbow, her neck straining to see past the ruins about her. But she could see enough.

"Oh no!" she exclaimed in horror. 'At least the distraction shield was still holding.' she thought thankfully. She knew this because outside the shield, a 100 or so Skree were amassed around the impenetrable dome, their reptilian eyes fixed on the beleaguered group; waiting, watching, guarding. 'Now, we are the prisoners!' she thought with another tinge of fright. The whole group had seen it now. Percival stood with his hands on his knees, leaning forward, breathing hard. Jazz and Chloe stood shell-shocked, eyes wide, almost afraid to move.

"Talk about out of the frying pan and into the fire," Sol said with a wry smirk, one side of his mouth raised. He saw the fear on the two girls faces and added. "We are safe in here, they can't get to us. The shield around the prison has not fallen completely." 'But they are getting out from somewhere?' he thought for a moment. Some distant sliver of a memory passed momentarily across his mind and then it was gone. "But where?" he said aloud.

"You know I talked about hope early on?" Percival asked. "Well, I think, now is a good time to remember that." he stopped when he realised no one was listening, although Sol was looking over his shoulder at him with a look that only a school teacher can give, by telling someone off without a word spoken.

Sam walked up to the very edge of the barrier, her heart thumping in her chest. Only a thin veil of magic stood between her and certain death. It was a very discomforting thought. The Skree that stood in front of where she stood, shuffled restlessly, reptilian eyes fixated on her every move. Not a word or sound came from their lips. She remembered how she had put her hand out through the barrier earlier and caught some raindrops, and she wondered if she did that now, what would happen. She had a good guess. In general, they stood a little taller than her, approximately five foot in height. Their bodies were not clothed, but were covered mainly in an armour of thin light green overlapping scales. Where there was none, the flesh was white and near translucent. Their faces were also scaled, from the head down, apart from a protruding snout that looked almost leathery in appearance. Their overlarge snake eyes, set either side of the snout, were a mixture of yellow and black, and it was this that made them look so inhuman. They shuffled about, slightly hunched over, on long arched feet, with claw like toes that matched the fingers upon their short but powerful looking arms.

"Can you understand me?" she asked the nearest one, her voice trembling. Its eyes blinked, its movements measured. The thing moved its head closer to where the invisible barrier was, eyes locked on Sam. Its thin lipless mouth twitched and a dark forked tongue flicked out, showing a row of thin razor-sharp teeth.

"Yessss," it almost spat. It sounded like what she would expect a snake to sound if it had vocal cords.

"What do you want?" she asked. She felt herself starting to look more and more at the lizard's eyes, which had somehow got larger. The cornea in the centre kept shrinking and then enlarging almost in sync with her own heartbeat.

"Why don't you come out here and we will show you?" it said. And a part of her agreed. 'Yes,' she said to herself. The eyes pulsed, in, out, in, out. Her legs felt shaky, her head light. 'What was happening?' she thought somewhere in the deep recesses of her young mind.

"Sam!" a shout came from what felt like a long distance away, but enough to break the spell. Sol reached her in an instant and grasped her right arm. Her eyes suddenly cleared and focused. She had stepped forward and was only inches away from where she knew the barrier was.

"Oh my goodness!" she said aloud. "He hypnotised me."

Sol led her back towards the group, but not before the thing hissed out a warning. "The Dragon will rise tonight and we will rule the Earth. Humans will be no more. You are too late to stop ussss."

"Everyone, please, don't get too close to the barrier and don't look into their eyes, they seem to have found a way to hypnotise people," Sol said to the group. "You OK now, Sam."

"Fine!" she said shaking a little. Sam reached her two friends, embracing them with tears in her eyes. "You OK, Chloe? What happened down there?" Sam asked, trying to take her mind away from what had just happened. Chloe instinctively looked back at the well, as if looking for something.

"I'm OK," she replied with a deep sigh, and then continued, "I was running and then something leapt from behind a pillar and knocked me flying. Before I could get to my feet, something grabbed me, and started pulling me further and further into the darkness. For some reason, I couldn't scream. It was awful! I fought back and then the thing screeched and suddenly let me go, its hand burning. The thing had gripped the cross by mistake, snapping it off my neck as it dragged me away. It dropped it and ran and I did the same, but I got trapped! The rest you saw ... "

"That thing ... the Shadowchaser saved you. It didn't harm you, it protected you, right Jazz?"

"I guess so," Jazz replied noncommittally, but she knew.

"They were wrong about it. I don't know how much they know and how much they are making up, but it's about time we found out," Sam said, looking towards the two Guardians, who seemed deep in conversation, oblivious to the situation they were in. But before Sam could act, Chloe gripped her two friend's arms tightly. "I want to try something!" Chloe said, getting to her feet. She walked around the fallen stonework towards where the moon shone and stood facing the shadow she had made on a large piece of upright rock.

"Come on out," she said aloud. Nothing happened. Sam knew instantly what she was trying to do!

"No, Chloe, don't do it," she shouted. The two Guardians turned as one and Sol was on his feet in an instant racing towards the girl.

"Chloe," he said in a calm manner. "That's not a good idea!" she ignored him. She had to know.

"Come on out," she said louder, but still nothing appeared. Sol reached her and started to pull her away and then suddenly something erupted out of the wall, bowling Sol over and pinning him to the floor.

"Woh, woh!" Chloe shouted to the creature. "He doesn't want to harm me." The thing stopped and Sol lay motionless, looking from the shadowchaser to Chloe and back. She knew he could possibly harm it, so she had to work fast, improvise.

"Please," She asked it, kneeling right beside it, raising both her arms, palms facing down, her eyes focused on the gleaming black facetted orbs atop the creature's body. And to her amazement, it stepped backwards off Sol and then scurried up the same rock and sat perched atop it, looking down at them, its glistening eyes catching the bright moonlight and reflecting it back at them.

"It understands you!" Sol said sitting up. "I had no idea, I never knew. I am sorry, it is only what we thought would happen, what we had read in 'the books of time.' It seems that that tale was wrong. It also seems like a new legend has been born today. You have a protector, young lady Chloe, and a good one at that," he said looking up at the thing and bowed to it. Its two front legs were beside its mouth, working the mandibles as if cleaning itself, but when it saw Sol bow, it stopped, looked at the group, then ever so slightly nodded its head once.

"Can I have one of those?" Sam said, smiling despite the fact that she was still shaking. The three girls hugged each other, smiling and laughing. Jazz looked up at the creature. "Just hugging," she said to it, and they all laughed again, a laughter of nervous relief that they were still alive more than anything else. And now that they were back on terra firma,

a thought occurred to her, a rational and sane thought.

"Our parents, they are going to go nuts? They must be out looking for us?" she said to the other two, but before they could reply, Sol interrupted.

"Time in here moves differently, it moves faster than out there. Do not worry, if we can sort out this little mess, we will have you home for tea in no time, won't we, Percy?" he said, with a little of his old charm back.

"A little mess! End of the world, a little mess?" Sam asked.

"We'll, you know, we have dealt with this before," he said nonchalantly.

"What with Arthur and his Knights, Merlin?"

"Precisely, and my name is no longer Merlin, that time has passed. Just call me Sol. It's easier that way. What have you got left Percival?" he said turning to the older man.

"The Witches' Candles are all gone, roman coins nearly gone. A torch. We got the sword hilt, thank the gods. Not much else apart from what I have in here." he said pointing to his heart. "Oh, and your journal," he said, handing it back to Sol. "And you?"

"Not much, this?" he held out something, a small purple pouch that seemed to have something bright within, before putting it quickly back in his pocket. "More coins

and ... "he pulled out something. "One more Witches' Candle." he said in surprise. "Didn't know I had that one!"

"We've got him?" a voice behind them said. They turned to see Chloe pointing to her shadowchaser.

"Yes, we have," Sol replied slowly with a bemused smile. "Yes, we have," he repeated. He looked at the girls and then back to the creature above him on the rock, another thought crossing his mind. 'No. I can't ask them to do that' he almost said aloud, before saying. "You need to rest, sit down and shut your eyes if you can. We have a little time on our hands. Conserve your energy, you might need it later."

"Why?" said Jazz, looking dismayed, hands on hips. "Haven't we done enough?"

"We have to stop Moribund and I'm afraid, we might just need your help."

None of the girls replied immediately. So much had happened so quickly. A roller coaster ride across and beneath the hills of Dartmoor had not been on their agenda that morning, but here they were, somehow still alive and intact. They each looked at the other, and then Sam turned to the two Guardians.

"Of course. But on one condition!" she replied, acting as the spokesperson for her group.

"And what might that be, Lady Sam?" Percival asked.

"We want to know what is going on. We have been following you like good little pupils, taking everything you say as the truth, all this magical stuff in our stride as if this was an everyday normal occurrence. Well it might be to you, but it isn't to us. You use magic! You swap minds! You have Magic Candles and coins! What else can you do?" she paused looking into their eyes, expecting a response, but they just stood there, giving nothing away externally. "Who are you, really?" she added to finish.

Percival let out a big sigh, looked at Sol, then smiled lowering his eyes. 'Something had passed between them again' Sam thought. Sol nodded and patted Percival on the back.

"Time to take these girls on a trip, Percy. Show them what they need to know."

"Be it on your head. Merl ... Sol," Percival corrected himself.

"Another trip!" Jazz exclaimed in dismay.

"Only of the mind," Sol assured them. "If you can all come and sit down, we will give you some answers."

The girls sat huddled together opposite the two Guardians forming a small circle.

"Now hold hands and shut your eyes please," Percival asked.

Sam shut her eyes, her left hand grasping Sol's large warm hand, while the other held Chloe's more dainty hand.

As soon as the circle of hands was complete, Sam felt a tiny jolt in her head and then she was somewhere else entirely. She opened her eyes and a scene of carnage confronted her. Instinctively, she gasped in fear. She stood atop a small rise upon what must still be the moor, but it looked so different, tree stumps and fallen trees littered the landscape. A massive body of water, a huge river, ambled through the hills, cutting through the countryside like a swirling paint brush, its reflection, burning red in the evening nights sky. Stones were scattered everywhere, and very recently, it looked to Sam. Bodies, human, Skree and other things she could not fathom, lay scattered amongst the ruined countryside, showing that a fierce battle had taken place. Weapons lay discarded or clutched in an icy hand of death. Smoke hung in the air and the taste of copper drifted on the wind. To her left a large circular fortress sat atop a crest, half destroyed, fires still ablaze within the ruins. Smoke wafted from the broken ramparts. Below her, four men stood with their backs to her, around a large stone plinth. Upon the plinth, three large ancient looking books sat upon the dais. One of the figures was talking in an almost musical incantation above the one opened book that lay in the middle, and as the person spoke so golden writing appeared upon the parchment like pages, as each word passed his lips. Even as he spoke, so the land itself began to change.

The ground shook beneath her feet and she reached out her hands for balance to steady herself. It almost seemed to Sam that the land was somehow righting itself. Boulders moved, rolled together, reformed. Trees reset themselves. The bodies upon the earth were swallowed up, drawn into the earth. The fires upon the battlements ceased. And then silence.

"The tomb is sealed," she heard the man say, in Percival's voice, closing the book. The scene stopped suddenly and she was back in the present. Before they could even speak, Percival started talking. His face looked strained and shiny with perspiration, the effort to show the girls obviously telling on his magical powers. They all knew what they had witnessed.

"We were not always prison guards you know. Once upon a time, we were and still are the Keepers of the Books of Time. The Books of Time show the three ages of man. We are in the second age of man. The third age, the age of enlightenment or damnation, is yet to be determined."

"That doesn't sound too encouraging?" Chloe asked.

No one bothered to reply to the retort, so enrapt were they.

"We have been fighting a war against the Skree since the dawn of mankind. The Skree are descendants of the dinosaurs; we humans are descendants of the Neanderthal. They evolved and settled in the hotter climates of the south, while man was born and survived in the frozen north. When men came down for the first time, from the snowy mountains into the green warmer pastures of the equator, the Skree at first welcomed them, then as more and more came, in fear, they turned on them and destroyed every man, women and child, vowing to wipe every human off the face of the earth, until, they alone would be left. By the end of the first age of man, before Atlantis sank beneath the waves and the wonders of man and the magic of the Earth was known to all, the balance was once more turning in favour of the Skree. But a great warrior king from ancient Valusia turned the tide and from then on, the Skree disappeared into the shadows, their numbers dwindled, but their hatred of man, instilled over the centuries, burned in their minds as they concealed themselves and plotted the fall of the human race. Over the course of history, mankind has held sway, few actually knowing that their hated enemy moved unencumbered amongst them, plotting, scheming, planning. Before the battle upon the moor, we were like you, we lived and died a normal life. Our brotherhood, the Keepers of the Books, had dwindled to only four. The books were passed down through the order over centuries, each one adding important details to help those that follow. Mankind's history is within those books as is the secret to Earth magic and how we use it. You know, in that time you saw, magic flowed through the essence of life as natural as the air you breath. It was that magic that made us immortal so that we could become the Guardians of the prison. We didn't even know until quite some time later." Percival paused, staring off into space, his features drawn into a rare smile of remembrance.

"There were four people around the books?" Sam asked.

"Yes, myself, Merlin, someone called ... "

"Lawrence Kane," Sam interrupted, remembering the name from the journal.

"Very good, yes. And ... Moribund."

"Moribund!" the three girls almost said in unison.

"I thought he was imprisoned?" Sam asked.

"That was the next time, when Arthur helped us," Sol interrupted Percival. "That was another close call, wasn't it, Percy?"

"Yes!" Percival replied, eyebrows raised. "Moribund was imprisoned then, he is a dangerous character. Little did we know we had been infiltrated at the highest level. Merlin, while studying the books, found the ancient words that only humans can say and those words are a powerful ally in our cause. The books, you see, are not normal books. You need to know how to decipher them, to be able to read anything, otherwise you are just looking at blank pages."

"What happened to Lawrence Kane?" Sam asked.

"Moribund destroyed everything that Lawrence held dear. Lawrence was the strongest of us all, the best magician, a true Warrior Guardian. He was, as you would call it today, a weapons specialist! Despite the fact that we are not meant too, Lawrence fell in love and let his guard down. It was a fatal mistake. He lost everything. He left the brotherhood and travelled the world on a mission to rid the world of evil, in all forms. He became a Champion of the Light and his escapades still filter through the history books to this very day, but under different names, of course. It was he that made the Witches' Candles that we use. He found that melting down a Witches' cauldron to make into metal wicks, then infusing it with wax and a little magic to bind it all together and hey presto, a candle light that would burn any Skree, close enough, to death while it was alight. You know already they hate the touch of metal in all forms. Hence the coins, the older the better. The properties that make up a Witches' cauldron are perfect for this purpose. It is the rawness of the metal that the Skree flinch away from."

"I think that is enough explanation for now," Sol interjected.

Sam looked to her friends again and they nodded to her, their faces a mask of determination, mixed with fear.

"You said you might need our help. Well, whether you like it or not, we're in, to the end," she added.

Sol smiled, knowingly, while Percival raised his eyebrows in astonishment at the girls' bravery, then said "Looks like we might have some new recruits after all."

Sam didn't quite understand what he meant.

"What's the plan?" Sam asked.

"We're working on it," Sol replied a little sheepishly. "Rest, please, as best you can. We will wake you, when it is time."

"OK, we will try," The three of them nestled down together on the moorland turf, taking comfort from each other's proximity and body warmth, their backs to the same stone that held the shadowchaser atop. Sam shut her eyes, feeling Jazz to her left and Chloe on her right. No longer did anyone fear the shadowchaser. Suddenly and unexpectedly, it had become a part of the group, a useful ally in this war against the lizard people. And before she knew it, nervous exhaustion took over and she drifted off to sleep.

She was standing on a single-track road, high up somewhere upon the moor, and somehow she knew she was dreaming. A distant stretch of water shone in the moonlight. It was a full moon, the light from it, giving the moorland an almost picture post-card snow effect. She didn't feel cold, despite a strong breeze that ruffled through the ferns and short cropped trees, but a shiver went down her spine when she saw what was stuck upon every branch and outcrop of vegetation. Even the rocks seemed covered in them as if everything had been wrapped in paper that had frayed over time. Countless snake skins could be seen for as far as the eye could see, rustling in the wind, making a noise that almost spoke to her, "Too late, you are too late," the voice of the moor said. She awoke with a start, remembering the dream, even as it started to cloud into her imagination. She knew the significance of it and shuddered at the thought. Her two friends were still dozing, and she heard the two Guardians in conversation, a few yards away to her left.

Without disturbing Jazz and Chloe, she pulled herself free and shuffled towards the voices, concealing herself behind one of the outcrops of ruins.

"Is there anything in the journal that might help?" she heard Percival ask.

"Only the inscription from the book I copied about the Dragon," she heard the rustling of pages. "From earth and stone, it will be made, from fire and water, it will rise," Sol's tone was inquisitive.

"The Dragon will have to be born from water, that is the glue that binds!" Percival answered with a hint of dread. "The Skree are free, the stones, the bones of the giant, will be brought together and Moribund has the power to resurrect it from the depths. We have to stop him, but we need to find out where he will bring the Dragon to life. They must have been moving the stones for some time now, moving them without our knowledge. It must be a large body of water. But where? If only we had a map of the prison, we could narrow it down. If it is set free, then nothing, nothing can stop it. Everything will be in vain. We have been complacent over the centuries, my friend, and I pray to the gods that we can make up for our mistakes, just one more time."

Sam gasped. 'Nothing can stop it!' Percival had said. 'Everything will be in vain!' she could feel a buzzing in her head. Her mind was racing. Something was gnawing at the back of her mind. A memory from this morning, but it was distant and her mind was feeling like it was about to explode. She needed to calm herself, so she returned her attention to the Guardians. Sol was speaking.

"To stop him, you know we need to get the Excalibur blade, unite the sword and then find out where Moribund is."

"Yes," was all Percival could say. "And you know what that means!"

"Of course. But how are we going to get past them?" he said, pointing to the Skree. "That's why they are here, to stop us getting out, and Moribund will be going for the blade as well." "He won't find it. Don't worry about that?"

"I could go for the car as a distraction, while you go for the blade," Percival said in a matter-of-fact way.

"Suicide! And we can't leave the kids here. They are with us now, and Chloe has a strong ally looking after her. We may need her and the Shadowchaser's help by the end of this. If only we had a few more, we could fight our way out. At the moment, we are going nowhere without a better plan."

"Let me go for the car, if I can get to it, I will be safe, protected," Percival pleaded. "It is my fault, I have to try." Sam had heard enough, her mind suddenly made up, a plan had formed in her mind, a mad one, she thought, but one that made sense to her.

She drifted back into the shadows and nearly jumped out of her skin, when she saw the other two girls coming towards her.

"That's the second time you have done that in a few days!" she whispered and directed them back into the ruins, with Sol's words ringing in her ears. 'If only we had a few more, we could fight our way out.'

Less than 10 minutes later, they appeared around the corner of the ruins and strode towards the two Guardians. Sol and Percival looked up and Sol was about to say something when he saw the look in their eyes.

"We have a plan," Sam said, her face a little ashen, but determined after what she had just done. "Chloe, the light please."

The two Guardians looked at each other and frowned. Chloe paced forward and put her hand out to Percival who handed her the torch, eyebrows raised in indignation. Sam and Jazz moved to their left, beside some taller rocks. And before the Guardians even had time to say anything, Chloe flicked the light on, casting two shadows across the mottled old stonework. Without a backward glance, Sam and Jazz clicked their fingers and to the Guardians utter astonishment, two more shadowchasers appeared out of the darkness within the rock. Both looked different to Chloe's, as if mimicking their host's appearances. These two dropped to the turf and sat behind them, gleaming black eyes fixed on the mass of creatures just beyond the shield. Chloe joined them and whistled to her shadowchaser, who scuttled down the rock and settled between the other two.

"Now, how about that for a plan," Sam said smiling.

Sol shook his head, a broad smile on his face. Percival just looked like he had seen a ghost, but rose and spoke to them.

"You are one brave bunch of girls', I'll give you that," They both knew what they had done to create these creatures. The two men then looked at each other, renewed hope now visible in their eyes.

"All we need to do is find out where Moribund is? A large lake or body of water, somewhere nearby?" said Sol, striding to the edge of the shield. The Skree shuffled back away from him. "The river is too shallow."

"How about the fishing lake?" Chloe asked. "The one below us."

"Still too small."

"The china clay pits, some of those have lakes in them." Jazz quizzed them.

"Still too small."

'Bigger!' thought Sam. And then the memory that had eluded her for a few minutes, just popped right back into her head as if it had been there all the time, just waiting for a prod. That morning, she had been sitting in her kitchen, having breakfast, speaking to her mum and watching the local news on television, when she remembered what the presenter had been talking about.

"I know where it is," she said, quietly, and then again louder, when they didn't hear her. "I know where it is, it's Burrator Reservoir," They all turned as one to face her. Sol clicked his fingers, pointing at her.

"Yes," he said confidently. "And they are coming out of the old tin mine entrance, right beside the reservoir. Brilliant, Sam." She smiled. "Now all we need to do is a get the blade and get there before Moribund raises the Dragon. What time is it?" He suddenly asked, out of the blue.

CHAPTER 9 -
TROLLSWORTHY WARREN

"There's too many of them! How are we going to get past them?" Sam whispered to Sol, watching as her breath formed in front of her. A sense of panic gripped her already tired and bewildered mind. 'It's getting colder and later!' she thought. They knelt, huddled behind a rock, 20 paces from a fast-flowing river. It had taken them a good time to reach here from the safety of the ruins. The plan was for Percival, Chloe and Jazz to head for the car, causing a distraction, thus allowing Sol and Sam to slip out unnoticed. She would never forget the first seconds, Percival running through the barrier, catching the Skree completely by surprise, bowling the first few over into more behind, causing mayhem. Chloe and Jazz had followed close behind, with the shadowchasers pouncing on any Skree that even moved towards them. Within seconds, they were swallowed up and out of sight among the throng.

At the same time, she felt Sol gently pushing her in the opposite direction, out into the darkness of the moor. They had been told that they must retrieve the blade before midnight otherwise "things would get complicated," Sol had said. "What kind of complicated?" she had not wanted to ask, but had. "Trolls come out after midnight," Sol had replied with a raised eyebrow, as if everyone on the planet knew it, except her. Once they had got the blade, Percival and the girls would have got to the car, and headed back to pick them up and head for Burrator.

At least 20 Skree paced in and around the river, moving across the barren landscape, sure footed and as silent as the wind. The way they moved, the snakelike way in which they flowed about the giant boulders, gave Sam the shivers. A sense of purpose could be seen among the group as they moved from one outcrop to the next, methodically checking every rock. A full moon, incredibly bright and close, cast faint shadows across the stone littered land-scape. Ferns covered the moorland floor, wavering in a gentle cold breeze, making it look to Sam as if the earth itself was moving.

"We are running out of time!" she added, when Sol didn't reply. All she could see of him was the back of his head as he peered around the edge of the rock. When he did turn to her, his eyes blazed un-earthly bright within the shadowed darkness of the overhanging rock. Sam almost shuffled back in shock, gasping as another rev-elation was suddenly thrust upon her.

"Your ... eyes!" she stammered out, a bit too loudly. Sol put his fin-ger to his lips, making a faint shushing sound.

"A product of longevity," he whispered nonchalantly. "Sorry, should have told you about those. Cool, eh? Happens when I am outside in the dark and the moon is out."

"What are we going to do? We are running out of time! It must be nearly midnight, by now, your time!"

"Two minutes to, actually." he said pointing at his watch. "They are moving away, going further upriver. They haven't found the White Stone. They don't know where to look. See, they have just walked straight past it," he said quietly, pointing in the direction of the river.

"It's in the river!" Sam exclaimed. "Didn't Moribund know that it was in the river?"

"It was once, in his day, beside the right-hand bank of the river near Trollsworthy Tor. But since mankind intervened and the local farmers decided to change the course of the river for their own ends, the stone has relocated to the centre of the river. I think that is one back to the 21st century, Mr Moribund," he smiled at Sam. Despite their predicament, she couldn't help but smile back. Sensing movement, he suddenly peered back over the rock.

"Oh no, they are turning back. We need to move, now," he said, taking her hand and starting to rise, but before he could, a huge roaring and rendering of rock, that made the earth itself shake, sent them tumbling for cover again. Sam pulled herself to her knees and peered back towards the cacophony of noise, to witness something she would remember all her life. On the hillside to the right of the river, Sam watched as giant boulders, started to uproot and roll towards each other, some coming down the hill, while others, rolled up the hill. As they closed upon each other, they clanked together like metal to a magnet. And gradually, two massive humanoid forms started to rise out of the landscape. First the squat head and giant shoulders could be seen. Moments later, arms as long as a bus were created and with these attached, the rest of the form was almost pulled, wrenched up out of the earth to stand upright, nearly 100 feet high, their shadows from the moon behind, covering the area where the two were hiding. The grey coloured stone looking forms were rounded with short stubby legs and bulging bellies. The hands had two fingers and a thumb upon each that looked as large as tree trunks. Thankfully to Sam, the faces were hidden by their own shadows, but when one of them turned sideways, she glimpsed a huge gaping mouth with row upon row of dirty thick teeth, that literally erupted out of the face. Sam's mouth fell open.

"Oh ... my ... goodness!" she said to herself.

"Trolls," was all Sol said, raising his eyes in dismay, as if he had just been handed a parking ticket. The Skree also stood motionless, transfixed at the sight. Not one had been knocked over or fallen, even with everything crashing about them, their balance and speed of poise was amazing.

"Well, well, well," one giant voice boomed, with a Devonshire accent. The one on the right, Sam thought.

"Three holes in the ground," the other replied. Sam couldn't tell the difference between the two voices.

"What have we here? I smell dinner, and it's not sheep, for a change, I smell Skree. Ain't 'ad a Skree for ages."

"They smell delicious," the other one said. They both leant forward, sniffing the air and peering at the Skree, who had still not moved. In fact, like a chameleon, they almost looked statuesque in the moonlight, as if by standing motionless, they might not be seen. Unfortunately, Trolls might not see very well, but their sense of smell was like that of any wild animal, honed to nature. And then the Trolls moved, belittling their size and girth, moving with incredible speed and agility, giving the Skree absolutely no chance to escape. In one giant sweep of its arm, the leading giant literally swept up four Skree in one hand and simply thrust them towards his gaping jaws.

"Don't look," Sol said sternly from her side, pulling her head to his chest. Above the sound of the Trolls movement and the steady roar of the river, Sam heard the faint screeching of terrified animals, a crunching sound and then silence.

And then all hell broke loose. A Skree appeared above them on the rock and leapt in the air, directly above their heads, trying to escape to safety. Suddenly a giant hand plucked it from the sky in mid-flight, even as the terrified Skree locked its snakelike eyes on the two hidden behind the rock. And then it was gone, snatched away. Sam tensed as one Troll suddenly stopped, the rumbling of the earth under its feet quietening as it stood motionless, barely five paces from the pair's hiding place.

"'Ang on a minute." it said "I smell magic. Magic is my favourite dinner."

Sam could hear it sniffing the air. Sol's eyes dimmed in palpable fear and he pulled them both closer into the rock. Barely a pace away from their hiding place a thin rivulet of water wound its way past them, idly weaving in and out of the ferns as it headed towards the larger river below. One pounding footstep moved closer to their concealment. Sam held her breath, squinting, her eyes closed for an instant before opening them again as Sol reached out with his left hand towards the tiny body of water. Inch by inch he stretched as another deafening footstep resounded in their ears. As his fingertips touched the water, Sam swore she saw a momentary faint luminance course out of his fingers and into the water.

"Eh!" she heard the Troll say. "That's funny! It's gone! Oi! Save some for me you greedy goblin!" the footsteps receded.

"Phew, that was close," Sol said letting out a deep sigh, while retracting his hand from the water.

"What did you do?"

"Water can camouflage the essence of magic. I dispelled some into the river. It put him off the scent, I am pleased to say."

"Me too."

They turned once more to watch, as the last Skree was hunted down and caught up by the other Troll. Even though the Skree were their enemies, Sam swallowed in fear with the realisation that none had escaped. The Troll that had been close to their hideout, now advanced on the other, intent on snatching the last hapless Skree. Suddenly they were at each other's throats fighting over the last petrified creature. "I've only 'ad seven" one said.

"That's your fault for going on a wild goose chase," the other replied. "Anyway, I caught 'im, I eat 'im," and proceeded to move the thing towards its mouth. Sam looked away again, as the second Troll caught the others hand before it reached its mouth and shook the thing free. In utter amazement the last Skree, dropped to the earth, landing nimbly on its feet and leapt into the river, in an attempt to escape to freedom.

"Now look what you made me go and do, you great big bumbling oaf."

"You can talk."

When the Skree reached the river, it spread itself and skimmed across the surface, like a water skier, sprang up the opposite bank and disappeared into the darkness of the ferns and boulders.

"Idiot."

"You're the idiot, I'm still hungry," one troll dropped to the floor sitting down no more than 30 paces from them.

"I'm quite full," it said rubbing its tummy. "I need a rest."

Sam looked towards Sol.

"Now, what do we do?"

Sol looked once at Sam, then back to the Trolls, before lowering his gaze to the floor.

"OK, here's the plan. Do you see that rock in the river, over there. The one that looks a bit like a hedgehog," he said pointing into the middle of the river, only 10 or so paces from where the seated giant's feet were resting. "That is the Mawnan stone. Beneath the surface, on the downriver side is a hole about a hand width in size."

"Hang on a minute. You're telling me this as if I'm the one who is going to get the sword piece?"

"That's because you are. Even with the water, they would sense something, smell something was wrong."

"Let me get this straight in my mind. You want me, a 13-year-old girl to go out there, get past two man eating Trolls, go into the freezing cold water, get wet and ... and what?"

"I haven't finished yet. If you hadn't interrupted, I would have told you by now."

"Carry on, just wanted to make sure that it was me you were sending out on this suicide mission, while you stay hidden safely behind this rock!"

"You are not going to die, don't worry. You just might get a little cold and wet though. Take this," he said, handing her a small gleaming charm he had taken from a tiny draw string velvet purse that she had noticed earlier. A thin black leather necklace held an oval, gold covered, glass Bauble. The thing gleamed and when it was placed in her palm, it pulsed and felt warm to the touch.

"What is it?"

"It's a ray of sunlight. Don't lose it and only use it if your life depends on it. It took me 300 years to catch that, you know. They're quite hard to catch, even when you know how to."

"How do I use it?"

"If the Trolls catch you, twist the bottom to let the sun out. Trolls hate sunlight."

"Like vampires?"

"Something like that. Oh, and shut your eyes when you do, it could blind you otherwise. Now, once you find the hole put your hand in until you feel the lever. As you turn the lever anti-clockwise, you must say out aloud. "Forsham tacckry melandast. Say it after me." "Forsham tacckry melandast."

"Very good, you could make a magician yet."

"That's if I survive the night," Sam answered sarcastically.

"You must say it loud enough, otherwise, the portal won't open."

"Hang on a minute! If I say it loud they are going to hear me."

"I'm going to leave my nice safe hideaway and lure them away from you," he replied with a smirk. "Anyway the sound of the river should muffle your voice. Pick up the sword blade and I will meet you back here. OK? Happy!"

"Delighted. I thought I was scared earlier, now I'm petrified."

"Good luck, I will be watching you, don't worry. I don't think your shadowchaser can help you, but you never know. Wait for my signal before going into the water, OK?"

"Thanks, I think I might need it."

"One last thing."

'More!' thought Sam.

"If either Troll farts, cover your mouth and nose as best as you can, it's been known to knock people out, you know."

"What?"

"Just wanted to make you aware, that's all."

With a shake of her head, she peered back towards the two Trolls. One stood statuesque 100 yards upriver, peering up and down the fast-flowing waterway for any sign of the last Skree. The other sat motionless, its head resting on a boulder, the odd loud belch, that sounded like a fog horn, erupting from its rotund face, being the only clue to denote that it was still awake. Sam watched intently and moved as soon as the standing Troll turned its head and peered up stream. She kept low, creeping from one piece of cover to the next, each time the Troll looked away. Every step, she looked as best as she could to where her next step would be. She drew within a few yards of the river, which was louder now, covering any noise she might make, and was more than pleased to see that a single-track path ran level with the river and below the line of the land, keeping her completely hidden from sight. The path like the river meandered away into the moonlight and towards the Trolls, and her destination. Used by the native livestock and local walkers, the path wound its way up and around boulders, past spindly half dead looking trees, while hugging close to the river, which gurgled and bubbled on its merry way towards the coast. She lost sight of the furthest Troll which was very disconcerting and every moment she expected to see a giant form loom above her, teeth gleaming in the moonlight. In places an eerie mist hung over the river. In others, ripples and eddies shimmered in the moonlight, like 1000 silverfish were beneath the surface. Inexorably, Sam crept ever closer until she turned a tight bend in the river and suddenly her heart was in her mouth. Barely a few paces above her and to her right, a giant foot rested atop a line of stones, literally covering the path she needed to take.

The foot was ginormous, at least 10 feet in length, with the heel of the three toed thing curving over the path to form a small tunnel. To her left and a little further upstream, Sam spotted her goal, a hedgehog shaped white stone, illuminated by the moonlight. It sat boldly alone, almost dead centre in the river, defying the elements. The river was approximately 20 feet across at this point and Sam couldn't tell how deep the water was, she just knew it was going to be cold! Mini-rapids caused eddies about the stone and others dotted along the river, changing the speed from fast to a meandering peaceful lazy flow. 'If the Trolls weren't here and it was daylight, this would be a magical place to be,' she thought, trying to regain her composure. She knew now that she just had to wait for Sol to act, before she went any further. She huddled under the shadow of a gorse bush and waited, one eye on the foot. Her mouth had gone dry, bone dry, and she couldn't remember the last time she had had a drink. Almost on cue, she heard the faint calls of a man. The foot moved, the heel dragging back dislodging small boulders and rubble, and one large gorse bush was flattened. The earth shook as she heard what must only be one of the Trolls, running across the stony landscape. It was almost like an everlasting earthquake as with each step, the ground shook. Sam instinctively reached out for stability and pricked her thumb on a gorse needle. "Ouch!" she exclaimed a little too loudly for her liking, clambering back undercover of the overhanging branches. 'OK, time to move,' she said to her aching limbs. Sam rose, hugging the bank, not knowing what might be only a few feet above her head and out of sight. Suddenly, the foot reappeared, crashing down into the same spot, literally, a few feet in front of her. Her heart would have jumped out of her mouth, if it hadn't been closed. It was then that the smell hit her; the foot reeked of the earth and a lot worse to boot. She pinched her nose and just kept going, her feet working despite every fibre of her being willing her to go in the opposite direction. Passing beneath the heel, she felt the coldness emanating from the skin and saw the thick veins of blood pulsing beneath. She felt sick, but thought that this was not the best time to 'chuck up', as Chloe would call it. She drew level with the stone that now gleamed in the moonlight, and nervously turned to see if she had been seen. Nothing moved.

Sam looked at the water and saw how clear it was. The moon was so bright that she could even see the smaller boulders and pebbles on the bottom of the river. A silverfish darted past, followed by a whole shoal of its kin. The water looked painfully cold. With one eye behind her, she knelt and dabbed her fingers in the river. She had already decided not to take her shoes and socks off, as she thought she might need to make a quick getaway at any time. The water was surprisingly warm, warmer than she thought. Without another thought, she turned and lowered herself into the water, as quietly as she could. It immediately came up to her waist and she was surprised to feel the pull of the current. Slowly and painstakingly, she waded out into the river, the force of its current threatening to betray her footing, with each movement. The rocky bottom was uneven and slippery, and many times she nearly lost her balance. Every step she looked back, and with each one, she saw more and more of the Trolls body. With each step she felt more exposed and couldn't help but peer back at every opportunity. And it was because of this that her lead foot slipped on a mossy stone and she went under with a splash and gurgle of bubbles. She felt the tug of the current again as she tried to right herself, but even as she started to pull herself out of the water, she saw the massive bulk of the second Troll standing over the river, peering in her direction. She thumped into a stone outcrop, reached out, found purchase and slid behind the cover of it before lifting her top half out of the water. Breathing in as quietly as she could, she peered around the boulders edge.

"I taught I 'eard somefing" it said to itself. And then it sniffed, once, twice. "I can smell 'uman blood" it said with glee. "Me likes 'uman almost as much as magic."

'My thumb!' she thought, wide eyed and quickly stabbed it under the water. The Troll sniffed again, while starting to lean back against the rocks.

"Think my nose is playing tricks with me tonight."

Sam let out a deep sigh of relief and peered upstream. The White Stone was only five paces away. The Trolls head leant back and Sam moved as fast as she could, fighting the current while trying not to make a noise above the sounds of the river. She reached the rock in seconds that felt like hours, and gathered herself behind it for a few moments. The Troll hadn't moved. She crept towards the bottom of the rock and started feeling under the water for an opening. In moments, Sam had located it and despite reservations of what might be hiding within, she started to stretch her arm into the hole. She had to lower herself, so that only her head was above the water. And when, she thought she could not reach any further, her outstretched fingers touched and grasped what felt like a metal handle.

'The words! Can't remember the words!' she thought in panic. 'Calm yourself, Sammy,' she peered back and thought she could see some movement from the Troll. That sight was enough to kick her brain into gear. The words came and she turned the key, speaking aloud. "Forsham tacckry melandast." Nothing happened. 'No!' she almost screamed. Again, she reached in, finding the handle and feeling that it had magically reset. She turned it again and spoke as loud as she thought she could. "Forsham tacckry melandast."

This time something did happen. The top part of the rock above the waterline split open with a crack, revealing an ancient rust encrusted sword blade. Sam reached in and picked it up, as she saw movement out of the corner of her eye. The Troll was rising, putting his hands to his stomach. Sam stood motionless, blade in hand, completely exposed in the water. The Troll however was not looking her way, but back up to the top of the hill. A low moaning could be heard from the beast as if he was in pain. And then it passed wind, with a noise that sounded like a fog horn from one of the tow tugs in the Plymouth Sound. And passing wind was true, as trees swayed and ferns were flattened. The sea of smell and rushing dirty air spread out towards Sam, who didn't know whether to laugh or scream. Sol's words leapt into her mind 'If a Troll farts, cover your mouth and nose as best as you can, it's been known to knock people out, you know.' The reminder was enough to make her act. Instinctively, she took a deep breath and literally threw herself under the water, her left hand holding onto the rock for leverage. Before her air ran out, a shadow covered the water and something gripped her left arm, yanking her out of the water and into the air, to stare face to face with the Troll.

"Taught I could smell 'uman. My nose is alright after all," he said over his right shoulder to the other Troll who was walking towards him.

"Couldn't find that slippery magician again," it said. "Ooh, what 'av you 'ere. Is that 'uman. I love 'umans, they're my favourite." Sam hadn't said a word. As soon as she had set eyes upon the Trolls eyes, she had been transfixed, and deep down, she now knew that this is how the Skree had felt. For the second time in one day, she lost her willpower. Once you locked eyes on the Trolls, it seemed impossible to do anything. They had a hypnotic stare that paralysed their victims, like a rabbit in headlights.

"It's mine and I'm going to eat it now, before you try and get your dirty 'ands on it, brother. You've 'ad loads already!"

With that, he proceeded to raise Sam towards his opened mouth. Sam's body caught the moonlight, casting a long grey shadow across the moor and river and out of that shadow a creature of nightmare erupted. The spider thing leapt from the darkness that had formed it, and it landed on the Trolls hand, blocking Sam's view, for the briefest of moments.

"Ahh, a spider!" the Troll screamed in absolute terror, instinctively flinging the thing off and letting go of Sam at the same time. Sam cartwheeled through the air, the spell broken, her senses returned, and shuddered when she thumped into another out-stretched hand, her breath leaving her with a whoosh.

"Thank you, brother." the second Troll smiled. "Looks like a nice little snack, this does." Sam saw that the shadowchaser had landed safely atop an outcrop of rock and was about to spring to her help, when the first Troll raised a massive boulder above its head with both hands and was about to bring it down, when Sam's hands clasped the necklace and without thinking, she shut her eyes and twisted the bottom segment, opening the bauble. She heard a sudden rushing of air and saw the backs of her eyes go white, and then silence and quiet. Sam opened her eyes. The Trolls stood motionless; they had been turned to stone! One still had its arms aloft, legs braced, stone in hand ready to throw. The one holding Sam had its face only a few yards from her and she could see that there was no sign of life left. She was suspended, 10 feet in the air above the moor. A stone hand held her loosely, so that she could wriggle free, swing off an outstretched finger and drop to the earth without too much bother, her gymnastic skills paying dividends at last.

She glimpsed her shadowchaser lurking in the shadows a few metres away. "Thanks," was all she could think to say, as it slinked back into the shadows. Movement to her right made her start. The blade was miraculously still in her hand. Sol appeared around the corner, clambered around a rock and stood staring at the scene, a sad look on his face.

"You used the ray of sunlight!" it wasn't a question. "I'm sure you had no other choice. Our need is certainly great," he said quietly, walking to the nearest stone statue and reaching up and touching it. "These were the last two Trolls living, you know. With their passing, the Troll race has run its course. I doubt they will be uni-versally missed, but it is sad to see them go, we have had many an adventure together, you know. Once a giant causeway stretched from one side of the valley to the other. This was all underwater. They lived under that bridge for centuries causing chaos and havoc to travellers, and continued living here even after it had turned to rubble," he looked around, peering into the darkness, then turned back to the stricken Sam. "We have time. Here, let me show you." he held out his palm to her. Sam placed her right hand on top of his and he followed it by placing his left hand atop hers; as if they were playing a game of One Potato, Two Potato.

As soon as his right hand touched hers, Sam blinked in utter amazement. She was standing atop a huge stone bridge that reached almost as far as the eye could see. A wide beautiful slow flowing river, ambled by below them. Tiny craft could be seen bobbing up and down in a gentle current, sails aloft. The sun was out, she could feel the warmth of the day and the smell of summer was in the air. The bridge was made entirely of boulders strewn together in a haphazard way, that somehow worked. A few carts and horses bumped up and down a short distance away, making an almighty racket. A huge eagle swooped past, gliding on a thermal, the width of its wings eclipsing the sun, moment-arily. People were walking up and down, on what must be a busy thoroughfare, she thought. In the distance gleaming spires silhou-etted against the horizon, denoting a large city. And then Sam looked closer as one group neared.

"Good day to you," she heard a voice speak. Sol's! But coming from her mouth! And then she realised, she was seeing this scene through Sol's eyes. Not all the group seemed human. One crea-ture hovered on translucent wings, gliding effortlessly across the rough terrain of the bridge. It was the size and shape of a human, but its features were somewhat different from its colleagues, who it kept astride of with the tiny fluttering of the wings that were attached to its back. The wings were almost translucent, showing a network of tiny veins and the light coming through the wings caused a rainbow effect upon the stones. The rest were human, but dressed unlike any she had ever seen, in clothes so brightly coloured that they made a rainbow look dim in comparison. Sud-denly a huge hand appeared from beneath the bridge to her left, a stone-grey hand with two fingers and one thumb. It reached up and grabbed the edge of the bridge and a Troll started to appear.

In one quick stride Sol hopped over towards the hand and gave it a sharp wrap with a staff, held in his left hand.

"Ow!" bellowed the voice, from below. Sol bent over the edge of the wall running along the length of the bridge and peered down, giving Sam a heart in the mouth moment of vertigo. The drop was 100 feet or more to the clear blue waters below.

"Now come on, Balstrom, no more please, there's plenty of sheep for you, so leave the people alone," the tone was light and said with a mild sense of annoyance. Behind him and seemingly out of sight, another giant hand appeared reaching over the stunned travellers, towards the unsuspecting Sol. Before he knew it, he was being lifted in the air by the scruff of his neck!

"We 'ave 'im now. " a second voice exalted.

"That is quite enough!" he said sternly, striking the two fingers with his staff. An electric blue current dispersed from the tip of the staff. Instantly, he was dropped to the bridge, where he landed daintily on his feet. He rose, ruffling his clothes back into shape.

"Now, you two know the rules, by now, you only eat the bad guys and sheep! Remember, you are meant to be the Gatekeepers, protecting the citizens, not eating them. You know what the enemy smell like, so stop annoying the people going about their everyday lives, especially me!" he shouted the last sentence, and brought the staff down on the bridge with a crash.

The image vanished. Sam was looking at her hand, clasped within Sol's. She looked up at the man who she now knew undoubtedly had been in this world for a long, long time, and was surprised to see his eyes were watery, a sad look on his face.

"All good things must end ... sleep well, my friends." He literally tapped the leg with the nail of his finger and immediately a myriad pattern of cracks appeared spreading across the whole figure, until when it reached the head, it started to fall apart and crumble. As this one fell, so it toppled upon the other, destroying it completely, the two Trolls falling as one, until nothing remained and the valley was empty, apart from the normal scattering of boulders that were associated with this area. Everything had returned almost to as it was, as if the Trolls, themselves, had been a figment of their imagination. Sam stood shell-shocked and for-lorn, not knowing what to do or say, a tear trickling down her rosy cheek. Sol looked at her and was also lost for words. In the end, he leant forward and put his arm around the young girl. She handed him the sword blade.

"I suppose we better go and finish this then," he said, giving her his best smile. "You know, you are an incredibly brave girl. Oh, did the Troll fart, by any chance?" he said trying to perk her up.

Sam forced a smile. "You could say that," as she saw over his shoul-der, the twin headlights of a car coming towards them. 'They made it!' she thought with relief.

CHAPTER 10 - THE DRAGON AWAKENS

Sam jumped in the back of the car and shut the door, delighted to see her two friends huddled together on the back seat. They looked a little shell-shocked and nervous, but pleased to see her.

"You've got some mud on your nose, Jazz," pointing at her friend's face. "Whatever next? Jazz with a dirty face."

"It's not mud!" Jazz replied, quickly wiping it away with her hand, but only proceeded in smudging it and making the mark worse, her eyes haunted with the recent experience. "Oh," was all she could say, realising what it was, and then added "It's good to see you." She put her hand out and they grasped it.

"Together forever," they all said, and grimaced.

Sol handed the blade to Percival, who looked at it, turning it over a couple of times in his hand, his thoughts his own. Sighing once, he looked up into the mirror, his blazing eyes looking at the group in the back. "How far to the dam?" asked Percival.

"Thank God for sat nav," Sol smiled, looking back at the girls with a wink, tapping the dashboard. He reached forward, pressed a few buttons and replied. "Four miles by winding road or one and a half as the crow flies."

"Then we better go as the crow flies, its quicker." Percival said with a tinge of excitement. "So, are we going to sprout wings then?" Sam asked in disbelief, although, by now, she could almost believe anything.

"Of course not, young lady, the car is. Did I not tell you the car can fly. Well, actually, the car can't fly, but the magic can make it fly."

"Percival!" Sol said loudly. "We are running out of time!"

Gaining his composure, Percival handed the sword hilt to Sol.
"I think this belongs to you, Merlin."
Sol also looked at the blade closely, then moved it closer to the
join on the hilt. Like a magnet, the two ends clanked together, the
break disappearing instantly. The rust started to drop off and disintegrate, falling like stardust, even as the silver handle started to
gleam. The leather bindings around the grip looked new, its ends
no longer frayed and hanging loose. Within moments, the sword
looked like it had just been placed there from the blacksmiths
forge, ready to use in its maiden battle. Ancient Gaelic writing
was inscribed upon both sides of the blade, and the moonlight
caught it momentarily as Sol twirled it in his hand, feeling the
weight of it, smiling as if it were an old friend.
"I want you to drop me off on the dam, as close to Moribund as you
can. You head for the old tin mine entrance and seal it. If I'm successful, I will be able to stop Moribund and seal the prison again,
all in one. If there are any Skree left out who haven't found human
form before sunrise, then we will rid the earth of most of them in
one foul swoop. You've just got to seal that entrance!" he said to
Percival.
"So, I think you had better take this," he handed him the Witches'
Candle.
"Oh, and take this, just in case," he handed something to Percival,
but in the darkness, the girls couldn't see what had been given to
the older man. "Now let's go."
Percival looked at the thing in his hand, his face sullen, then back
at Sol. Something passed between them then, a knowing bond
almost older than time, an unspoken truth that only they knew.
Sol smiled and swallowed, then forced a better smile for the girls.
"Come on, Percy, let's get the old girl going," again he turned back
to the girls. "Everything is going to be alright," he said, his face
drawn with a false smile that did not reach his eyes.
"Now listen up." The engine started. "Oh, and you'd better buckle
up too. Don't want your parents having a go at me! I am going to
stop Moribund and reseal the prison. This sword has the power
to do that. I want you and Percy to close the entrance, to seal the

Skree outside." he looked at his watch. "We have less than an hour till sunrise. Any Skree not in human form by then will perish. The sun will destroy them."

"Like vampires." Chloe said.

"Something like that!" he replied with a smirk. "The only problem is you three humans and Percival, will be the only ones in their way to stop them, so you will have to be strong, one more time, please."

"We are not alone," Jazz spoke up, defiantly. "We have our shadow-chasers."

'And you're going to need them to survive this night.' he was going to add, but thought better of it.

"Yes, yes you do." was all he could reply.

Suddenly the car lurched and then righted itself. "Oops, sorry. I did not see that gorse bush," Percival said from the driver's seat. To the girl's utter amazement, they suddenly realised that they were airborne, gliding in the air, a few feet above the moor. The lights of the Range Rover shone forward into the night's sky picking out any obstacle jutting out of the silhouetted landscape. They had not felt a thing, never felt the car even rise, but now that they were aware of it, they could feel the very gentle swaying to and fro, almost as if they were sailing on water. As if reading their thoughts, Percival said

"It's a bit like sailing a boat, you know. The wind is like the sea, you just can't see it, unless you know how to. The faster it goes so the currents change colour, almost like looking at a moving rainbow. To go faster, you ride the darker coloured currents and to slow, you simply move gradually towards the lighter tones. You see." While he was speaking, so he was steering the wheel and they could feel the ebb and flow, the increase and decrease in speed. But Sam could see no wind, and especially not any different coloured wind. They felt the car lurch as they crested a bluff and suddenly flew off the end, leaving the dark earth far below.

"The higher you go, the harder it is to control, as there are more and more currents beneath you that affect the particular current, which you are riding on. There is a knack to it, you know," he looked across at Sol for approval, but his head was lowered deep in thought. Sam could only just see the side of his head, but she could see that his lips were moving in some silent prayer. And somehow then, she knew.

"You're not coming back are you?" she said. His lips stopped, then he raised his head, stretching his head back, before eventually turning to look at her.

"I hope so, Sam, that's all I can hope for. You know we can't die."

"Unless killed by fire and steel, water and wood … "

"Thank you, Percival," Sol interrupted with a wry smile. "Look, ladies, a lot rests on what we do in the next hour. If sacrifices have to be made, then it will be for the greater good. I am tired. A 1000 years or so can take a lot out of you, trust me. I have lived a great many lives, seen wondrous things, many evil things, but always the goodness of man prevails. It is our duty to make sure this continues … " Sam undid her seatbelt leant forward and put her arms around Sol's neck. He reached up one hand and placed it on hers. She felt the coldness of a tear roll down her cheek against the warmth of the man's head. She hardly knew him, but somehow, she knew that this one man had done so much over the centuries to protect this world, and no one, except her and her friends, would know this truth. Only in legends and fairy tales would the stories be told now.

"There she is," Percival said interrupting the reverie. "Burrator Reservoir."

They were amazingly high up now, what felt like hundreds of feet above the earth, flying over a large canopy of trees. Through the windscreen, the moon cast an eerie glow across the surface of Burrator Reservoir. The dam was just visible, a dark mass of stones cutting a swath across the moonlit waters. The girls had all been to Burrator many times together and knew the single-track road that cut across the top of the dam with its low wall on either side. Sam knew that Jazz was scared of heights and hated crossing that bridge. Percival dropped the car lower and swept left past the dam. It was then that everyone started to see movement among the trees, movement everywhere. For as far as they could see, 1000s of Skree stood in, and among, the trees, waiting and watching the lake. Sam remembered her dream from the ruins, of the large expanse of water and the fluttering in the wind of the 1000s upon 1000s of shed lizard skins and she gritted her teeth, feeling the icy tendrils of fear dancing up and down the nerves in her spine. 'This is it!' she thought. They passed over the edge of the lake and saw a single boat bobbing up and down in the middle, a solitary figure standing in it, arms aloft. 'Moribund' thought Sam. He seemed to look up towards the car, but Sam wasn't sure.

The car passed over the lake, gliding close to the water now, its moon cast shadow racing across the water in its wake. And then Percival called out "there!" he said pointing. Set back, just across a road that wound around the lake through the trees, a large wedge of rock had been cut out of the hillside. A huge cavernous opening that marked the entrance to the old tin mine was cut into the rock and had been sealed off for many years, until now. The large fence with the 'Danger Keep Out.' sign had been torn down and trod upon by many feet. Pouring out of the darkness were more and more Skree, a moving mass of shadows bursting forth from their centuries old prison. Within the throng, they could all see that groups of 20 or more were carrying huge boulders towards the lake. As Percival, banked and turned towards the dam again, they saw one group cast a large boulder into the shimmering waters. With a splash it sank out of sight into the depths. Another group approached and repeated the act, and then spread out and stood watching the silent water.

"That was the last one," Sol said. "We have still got time, Percival" he added.

"I am on it, as you youngsters say," he glided across the lake again, turning and banking so that he was running level with the top of the dam. Ever so slowly, he lowered the vehicle towards the road. The girls' mouths were agape, their stomachs protesting at the sight before them.

"No way," Chloe said, between excitement and fear. One wrong move and they could either end up in the reservoir or tumble over the side to their doom and into the concrete darkness below the dam. The car glided down just as if it were a plane and even as its wheels touched the concrete, Skree were emerging onto the dam from both sides. With a juddering brain rattling bump, the whole car gripped the asphalt and skidded to a halt, but instead of stopping the car, Percival started to accelerate towards the nearest Skree and to the girl's horror, bowled them off the dam, as if they were ten-pins. The creatures did not seem to strike the vehicle, but seemed to just fly off in every direction within close proximity of it. Once he had cleared the far end, he screeched the brakes on and spun the back end of the car around as if on a six-pence, to face back down the dam and in the direction of the tin mine.

"Where did you learn to drive like that?" Sam asked impressively.

"Le Mans, 1963, actually," he replied over his shoulder. To Sam, Percival actually seemed to be enjoying this, as if this was what got him going. The sense of fear, the feeling that great things were at stake seemed to motivate him, and she wondered how many times this type of thing had happened. As they neared the centre of the dam, Percival slowed down and Sol opened the door, sword in hand.

"Good luck, my friend," Percival said solemnly, and they clasped hands.

"You too," he turned and smiled at the girls one last time, then shut the door. "Go," he shouted to them.

Percival floored the accelerator as more Skree raced towards them, only yards away now, their numbers covering the whole road from side to side. Sam gulped in awe and fear. The car sped forwards and ploughed through them. This time the sheer numbers did force the car to slow and they could feel the impacts now. In the mirror as they sped away, a few Skree that had escaped the car converged on Sol, who swung the sword in a massive arc that turned any Skree, within contact distance, immediately to white dust. In the car, it had turned dark with the number of bodies around the vehicle, but still they came on.

"Come on, old girl!" Percival shouted to the car and it rose, clearing the masses upon the dam, almost leapfrogging above the main body of them, upon the road, before landing and crashing with another bone crunching bang into a tree.

"Out, quickly," he said a little dazedly. The three girls bundled out.

"This way," they ran along the road towards the tin mine, with a thin line of trees to their right between them and the reservoir. Scattered within the trees, Skree stood facing the lake, oblivious and suddenly uncaring to the four humans running behind them. Sam peered back across the water towards Sol and could see him fighting, swirling the sword and forcing the Skree back, time and time again. More and more of them amassed behind their fellows ready to take on the human with the gleaming sword. 'It would only be a matter of time!' Sam thought in panic. Through the trees and visible in the lake, Moribund was shouting something. The Skree, en masse, started to pound their feet in unison, the noise deafeningly loud enough to make the earth shake as if a handful of Trolls had just arrived for the party.

In the middle of the reservoir, the waters began to boil, huge bubbles rising to the surface and bursting. Towards the dam end, a large piece of stone, bigger than a house started to gradually lift itself out of the water. The group raced along the road and stopped opposite the broken-down fence to the tin mine, watching the scene unfold.

Sol stood on the bridge, leaning on his sword, his arms weary and aching with the continual lifting and swinging of the heavy blade. 'I am out of shape!' he said to himself with a smirk, 'just hang in there a bit longer, and then I can rest.' he thought again with a wry smile. The Skree had backed off momentarily, their gaze now towards the lake, as before him the Dragon started to appear out of the water. The head appeared first, its huge gaping jaw open and wide, its rows of teeth dripping wet and glistening in the moonlight. One tooth was the size of one boulder, so large was the Dragon. Water cascaded down from the opened mouth and rolled off the head in torrents. Moribund was sat above its scaly neck and when he saw Sol, he screamed "kill him!" towards the Skree.

Sol's sword was up in an instant, impaling the first one that had crept up behind him and cutting a swath through three more to his right. A body bundled him off his feet to crash into the wall between the water and the road. The sword slipped from numbed hands and started to topple over the wall. His breath was knocked from him and he looked up into the eyes of the advancing Skree. He shouted a word and the sword stopped its descent and shot to his hand, just as the first Skree reached him and died on its tip. Placing his back to the wall for support, he rose and swung the sword in a wide arc, scattering the Skree a few yards back. He turned and climbed atop the small wall and stood facing the emerging, huge, Dragon. By now, its massive shoulders had started to show above the frothing waters, its long stone-like scaly neck lifting the head almost above the tree line. Wing tips emerged, covering the whole width of the reservoir, the wings themselves causing tons and tons of water to pour off and cascade back into the reservoir with an almighty crash. Suddenly at the other end of the water, a bulbous looking tail appeared, flicking to and fro. Sam had never seen anything so large that moved. The thing blotted out the moon, covering the banks in dark shadow. 100s of tons of water constantly dropped off the thing as it started to free itself from its own prison, causing the waters to foam, as if the water itself was boiling. Huge reptilian eyes opened on either side of its 40 foot snout. Sam and the girls said nothing. They were genuinely speechless. Everyone was watching the birth of something that had not been seen by human eyes for 1000s of years. As each part of its body was exposed to the air, so the stone look changed to a mottled fluorescent, green scaly skin. Waves crashed upon the shoreline, washing some Skree off their feet. Sol looked into the jaws of certain doom, watching as the stones inside the huge mouth changed form, becoming fleshy and lifelike. 'The water is the glue that binds.' he remembered Percival saying, and then he knew what to do.

Moribund looked down upon the tiny figure on the bridge and smiled at the futility of the man. 'Nothing can stop me now,' he thought, just as Sol raised the sword above his head in both hands, tip down. He braced his legs, took a deep breath and brought the sword down with all his might into the stone bridge.

"You shall not rise!" he shouted. The sword entered the solid stone like it was going into soft earth, driven in all the way to the hilt with every ounce of power that he had. He let go and the handle vibrated to and fro. Nothing moved, even the Dragon had stopped, it's massive red bloodshot eyes staring at the bridge. And then a crack appeared, small at first, followed by another, forming a myriad of interlacing cracks. A rumbling from beneath the bridge made the ground shake, throwing the Skree to the floor in fear. As Moribund looked on, vein like cracks began to form on the inside of the dam, above and below the water line. A few bubbles popped to the surface.

"No!" Moribund screamed.

Sol smiled and turned his head towards the enraged magician. "Not tonight you don't, not tonight."

And then the dam burst, the pressure of the water too great for the cracks that had appeared. The whole end of the dam just collapsed in on itself, a tidal wave of onrushing water taking the Skree, Sol and the sword down into the depths below. With a roar, the water raced through the opening forcing more of the dam to collapse. The Dragon shook from side to side its legs not fully formed, tottering on stumps, as if walking for the first time. Cracks appeared upon the legs and body, before starting to crumble apart from the bottom up. The head peered backwards before turning and opening its mouth, roaring once in defiance, a roar that made the trees bow. The shoulders and head started to collapse in on itself crashing forward into the escaping waters and disappearing into the frothing depths. Moribund was thrown from the shoulders, crashing into the diminishing reservoir's waters beside the bridge, bobbing up once, clinging to the side of the ruined dam momentarily, before being dragged beneath the surface by the powerful undertow. Sam and the group stood rooted to the spot, watching the whole thing unfold.

"No." She said, her lips quivering, tears forming in her eyes as she saw Sol thrown into the swirling landslide of mud, stone and water. As she watched, she saw the sword, still stuck in a large chunk of rock, cartwheel over and over before also disappearing into a mist that was forming above the raging torrent. A hand on her shoulder made her jump for the third time in two days. She looked into the pensive and sad eyes of Percival.

"Come on, we must go, our job is not finished yet," he said to them all.

"Sol!" was all she could say weakly.

"I know," he replied "but we must seal the entrance."

A noise in the trees in front of them between the road and the emptying reservoir broke their reverie. As if broken from a trance, the Skree started to turn and move as one towards them, the closest, barely 15 yards away.

"Quick, this way," Percival shouted, forcing the stunned girls through the trees towards the mine. The girls ran for their lives, feeling the vibrations of the Skree as they stampeded towards them. Whether they were heading for the safety of the mine or after them, Sam knew not, she just knew that they were right behind them moving at breakneck speed. They slowed as they fought their way through some vegetation, their clothes snagging on brambles and whipping free all in the same instant. Out of the corner of her eye, Sam spotted a movement above her in the branches and screamed a warning. 'The Skree were flying through the trees outflanking them!' she thought in fear. A dark shape with red eyes hopped from one branch to the other and sprang at Jazz. Jazz turned, arms outstretched for protection, even as out of the shadows, a shadowchaser appeared, catching the thing only feet from the young girl's head and casting it away into its advancing companions. 'The shadowchasers were obviously at home in the branches too,' Sam thought with a sigh of relief. She looked for hers but could not see it in the trees.

More Skree appeared in the trees above, eyes gleaming, their bodies poised for action. Percival stepped in front of the girls and uttered some words that sent the closest scampering back, hissing and snarling in annoyance. Behind them, Sam spotted the broken fence and just beyond, over some open ground, the dark opening

THE DRAGON IN THE STONE

to the mine. They raced towards the entrance and turned to face the oncoming throng. The moon was still visible, but a faint light in the sky signalled that the beginning of a new day was just over the horizon. Out of the shadows, upon the wall behind the girls, the three shadowchasers crept forward and stood in front of the them, waiting. Sam picked up a large piece of wood, handed it to Jazz and then found another piece for herself. Chloe picked up a couple of rocks and held one in her left hand, weighing it for feel. A massing throng of the things, true worms of the earth, crept forward, forcing them back, step by step.

Percival looked at his watch. "10 minutes till dawn " he said, "We have 10 minutes to hold out." He turned to the hole in the rock. It was massive, about 40 feet high and at least 20 feet across, large enough to get the heavy machinery in that was needed for the tin mining. Now it was just a yawning mass of darkness that led to the prison beneath the land.

"The sword has returned to the earth and sealed most of the prison. In time the magic will spread and encompass all of it, but not yet ..." he told the girls. He was almost skittish now, darting his eyes ahead of them and then back behind them into the inky blackness of the tunnel. "There are more coming out," he said sullenly. "I need to close the tunnel now," he said to himself in a matter of fact way. 'The candle will destroy it, but then the girls will not survive' he thought.

In front of the girls a moving mass of Skree stalked towards them from all sides, and they involuntarily stepped back with Sam bumping into Percival. They locked eyes and he smiled, the 'Sol' smile that said 'I'm not coming back and goodbye', all in one. The Skree moved forward with every step that they took back. The group started to rise towards the entrance, back-pedalling with the shadowchasers scuttling back with them. For as far as she could see, Skree littered the area in front of them in their 1000s. "Ok, if I don't come back, you need to make your way back to the stone with the hole in, step through it and walk clockwise seven times. That will bring you back to the normal present time. If we are successful, everything will be as it was and you will be home ... " he looked at his watch. "Nearly in time for tea. Seek out Lawrence Kane, he will help you, show you the next step. Give him this, he will understand. You are the Guardians now if I do not return." Something small and cold was pressed into Sam's hand. She stared wide eyed at Sol's ring.

"There is great magic in that, do not lose it. Give it to Lawrence, OK. He will explain. And please, make him take you to the fairy market and stag race. If I can't be there, he must! Remind him please. It is important!"

Tears were falling down her cheeks now. First Sol, now Percival. How were they going to survive for the next five minutes and beyond, without him, without Sol? So many unanswered questions, so little time. It wasn't fair. Her thoughts returned to Sol, trapped forever under tons and tons of rock and water, never able to get out. She thought of Excalibur, stuck in the rock, falling over and over into the chasm. She saw the rocks of the Dragon disintegrate before her eyes, and crash back into the fast draining reservoir. She saw Moribund tossed off the back of the Dragon to be consumed by the frothing dirty waters, a scream of abject hatred piercing the swirling depths.

Her reverie was broken as Percival withdrew the last Witches' Candle, uttered a few Gaelic sounding words and rolled it in front of them. The thing erupted in a blinding flash of blue light, bathing the area in an unnatural bright light that sent the Skree cringing away into the shadows. The candle stopped just past the shadowchasers, who seemed totally oblivious to its powers over the Skree. The light emanating from it covered the entrance and a few yards in front of them. The group stood in the light, bathed in the warm glow of the candle's magic, looking out at the advancing throng. For the moment, the Skree were not going to approach that light, they were too fearful of the consequences. But already, even as Sam looked, she saw the candle begin to dim and flicker.

"Fight well, my young friends and a good life to you," Percival strode to the back of the entrance, just as the first Skree appeared from within. With a word of magic, he sent it scurrying back into its brothers behind him and without stopping he started to call out in a loud voice. He placed his hand on one side of the entrance, and then raced across to the other side. A rumbling started to sound deep in the earth. He placed his hand on this side, and then strode back to the middle. Suddenly a Skree pounced on his back from the darkness, another two followed close behind.

"Percival!" Sam screamed. He somehow flung them off and raised his arms wide to the cavern's roof, shouting again in the ancient tongue of his forefathers. A horde of Skree jumped towards him, but never got there.

A loud cracking sound was followed by tons and tons of falling stone. The ground shook, and a billowing dust cloud spread out from the tunnel encompassing the three girls, the shadowchasers and surrounding Skree.

As it cleared, so Sam saw that the entrance was completely sealed by fallen rock. A maddened screech of fear erupted from the Skree, a sense of panic palpable in their movements as they paced about. Suddenly, they started to fling themselves towards the entrance as if they could somehow find a way through. Some screamed as they made contact with the light of the candle, but still ploughed on, regardless. Others came rushing at the girls only to be stopped in their tracks by the shadowchasers quick movements and powerful legs. But even the shadowchasers could not stop them all. One lurched above Sam and she squatted at it like a fly, feeling the force of the blow strike the thing square across the head, knocking it sideways and into the welcoming arms of her eight-legged ally. She looked away, a brief glance towards the sky and horizon. 'Come on' she thought, pleading to the sun. Another movement to her right and she cartwheeled out of the way as a Skree pounced at her. She rose and stood facing it, legs outstretched, weapon held out. She looked down. The weapon, a piece of wood was now half the size and no real weapon at all, it had snapped off with her last encounter and she hadn't noticed this. Out of the corner of her eye, she saw Chloe, back to back with Jazz, throw her stone and remarkably strike the nearest Skree. Jazz was swinging the stick back and forth in front of her, keeping one Skree at bay until her shadowchaser came to the rescue. One shadowchaser landed on the floor close in front of them, one of its hind legs broken and snagging on the earth. At the same time she saw Chloe yelp and start to hobble on her left as if she had been struck. Sam instantly realised the truth. If the shadowchasers are hurt, so it transfers to the host human. Her eyes widened as the Skree facing her, pounced. She knelt curled and rolled under its advance, came up early and threw the remainder of the wood at the thing's back. It yelped, turned and in an instant was upon her. She fell backwards to the earth, feeling the cold clammy hands at her throat and the weight of the creature on top of her, its blazing red reptilian eyes, flickering with triumph. She was pinned and couldn't move. She felt the hot fetid breath of the thing that had lived almost all of its life beneath the ground, and she tried to fight, to free herself, but it was to no avail. She shut her eyes, waiting for the inevitable and then suddenly, the weight was gone, the hands around her neck gone, the feeling that something was pinning her down, gone.

She opened her eyes and they watered instantly as dust caused her to wince and choke when she took a breath. She sat up and looked around. For a moment, she couldn't believe her eyes. She could not hear anything at first, her senses numbed, her mind in a vacuum of confusion. A faint light was filtering through the trees, casting dewy shadows upon the ground amongst the trunks. She felt the warmth bathe her face and a cool wind ruffle through her tangled hair. White dust was everywhere, billowing in the wind all around her, in and beneath the trees, covering the underbrush and the road in the distance. She looked at her clothes. She was covered in it! And then it dawned on her. 'This was what was left of the Skree, when the sun rose,' she brushed it off fraily, as quick as she could. Her hearing returned just in time to hear a familiar voice.

"Er, Gross!" Jazz exclaimed, brushing some dust off her clothes with the edge of her fingers in disgust. The shadowchasers were nowhere to be seen. Chloe, who was also on the ground, clambered to her feet and started dusting herself off. She clutched one leg and rubbed it with a grimace on her face.

"Just like vampires," she said looking at Sam with her lopsided grin.

'How could she laugh at a time like this?' Sam thought. She peered around her in shock at the entrance, sealed forever by the valiant Guardian, Percival, who was trapped beneath. "Percival," she said shaking her head, remembering his final words. "You are the Guardians now, if I do not return."

'Us! The Guardians.' she thought looking at her two friends, with a faint smile.

"OK, Percival, we will do our best, I promise," she said towards the mine opening. They walked in a daze through the cloud of white dust until they reached the place where they thought the Range Rover had struck the tree. Sure enough, there were marks upon the tree where something had hit it, but the car was gone, only three bikes lay upon the forest floor. Without a backward glance they clambered upon their bikes and started off towards the cairn of stones. The cycle back was surreal, the waters were still flowing out of the broken dam, but it was just a steady flow now. Not a single bird sang its dawn chorus. Even the ponies, sheep and cattle were nowhere to be seen. It felt to Sam like they were the only living things on the planet, so encompassing was the silence. It almost felt as if the world itself was holding its breath. They reached the base of the hill below the cairn, dismounted and raced up to the ruined fortress. Reaching the stone with the hole in, Sam ushered Chloe, then Jazz through, before something out the corner of her eye made her glimpse through the ruins to the top of the hill. Just for an instance, two white clad robed figures stood upon the silhouetted horizon looking down at her, but when she turned to get a better look, so they began to shimmer and disappear. She put her hand up above her eyes for a better view, blinked in the sunshine and they were gone. She knew those figures, knew the way they stood, the size and shape of them. She smiled, looked once more at the ruins about her and clambered through the hole. As Sam finished her last backward step, a sudden feeling of air escaping from a vacuum whooshed about her, followed by a moment of silence, then she opened her eyes wide to see her friends looking at her, big smiles on their faces, arms entwined. She felt the warmth of the sun again on her back, but this felt different somehow, warmer than before and the wind itself felt less biting. The ruins were gone, only the cairn and the stone remained. A brown and white pony wandered by nibbling on the grasses of the moor. Behind it, more ponies were interspersed with sheep, all happily going about their normal grazing.

"Look at the time," Jazz said in amazement.

Chloe beat her to it. "It's only 6.26!"

Sam looked at her watch as if she didn't believe it, knowing full well that it was true, even before she saw it.

"Did we just dream all that?" Jazz asked.

Sam's hand felt something in her pocket and removed it. "I don't think so," as she opened out her hand to show them the ring nestling in her palm.

Epilogue 1

Sam left her friends at the crossroads and cycled home, her mind a mixture of amazement, sadness and exhilaration all mixed into one. As she entered the house, her mum looked her up and down, before giving her a big hug.

"You know I'm so glad you went to Exeter today. Did you hear that there was a landslide at Burrator and the dam nearly overflowed. They had to close the road across the dam you know, and I know you guys often go up there. Just glad you weren't anywhere near. They say a lot of rubble has been falling into the water and that is why the water levels have been rising. The old tin mine had been crumbling and falling into the water. Today, the whole front entrance collapsed. It's all cordoned off now. They are lucky the dam hasn't burst! After all that's happened recently, I shudder at the thought of you three being up there, you could have got yourselves into some serious trouble."

Sam was shaking her head inwardly. She smiled. "You don't know the half of it, mum." she held onto her mother a bit longer, trying to control her emotions. When she had gathered herself, she let go.

"That was a big hug," her mum said with a wry smile, eyebrows raised. "Are you sure you're OK?"

"I'm fine, just a bit tired. It's been a long day!" she smiled again, feeling the ring in her pocket. And a thought crossed her mind. 'I wonder who Lawrence Kane is, and how am I going to find him?'

* * *

Dawn was breaking across the edge of Dartmoor, the land warming to a new summer's day. The sun broke across the low hills casting a long ray of brightness through the countryside and across the placid waters of the reservoir. Birds sung their dawn chorus and the native creatures of the moor started to rise and feed off the grasses and vegetation. Dew hung heavy on webs spun in the dark of the night, making them look like they were made from glass by the hands of pixies. Darkness still hung in the shadow of the trees surrounding the water, the sun not high enough yet to penetrate though the holes in the canopy. A disturbance on the edge of the water caused a squirrel to drop its nuts and scamper up the closest tree to safety. A ripple in the water pertained to something beneath. A dirtied black tentacle broke the surface and reached out for the shore, grasping the nearest tree, followed closely by others. A large rounded head within the centre of these tentacles, burst forth, its features bloodied, bruised and covered in mud and slime. The thing roared an inhuman scream of vengeance from deep within its soul, before pulling itself up and out of the water, to lie face down on the grass, the body a mass of human and tentacle. A dove alighted from a branch nearby and flapped away across the lake and into the wood opposite. Moribund lay there, feeling the warmth on his back, the waters draining away, his tentacles returning to him, their job done. He concentrated and rose to kneel, his body changing even as he moved. The mud and slime dropped off, the face rippled and contorted, the clothes that were ripped, shredded and dank; shimmered and changed, and became clean and new. He began to stand, his bones creaking as he straightened and even before he took his first step, the thing that had come out of the lake, was gone and in its place stood a man.

'Free,' he thought, with a hint of joy, and he strode forward. 'They might have stopped me this time, but I am still alive, I will seek my vengeance.'

He reached the first line of trees and started through them towards the road, feeling the soft mossy soil beneath his feet. He approached a narrow bend in the road and stopped there, his right hand to his head in thought. 'I sense that Merlin and Percival are trapped beneath the earth. Hah.' he thought, with a smug smile. 'No one to stop me now, except those pesky girls and the apprentice, wherever he might be. I will find them and destroy them, then I will have all the time in the world to plan, oh what a lovely day it is today.' He said to himself with a sinister grimace.

"Hey, Moribund!"

"??!!!" Moribund looked behind him, the voice instantly recognisable. 'Merlin's!' he whipped his head around, but there was no one there. Only the silent trees stared back at him unmoving.

"Hey, Moribund. Over here." Percival's voice came to him from everywhere and nowhere. He swung around confused, a look of absolute hatred drawn across his features.

"Hey, look behind you." He turned again, just in time to see the shiny grille of a massive 20 ton log lorry, bearing down on him. His eyes didn't even have time to rise fully, a mouth half opened, a moment where he recognised the sound of a horn and the screeching of brakes, and then he was hit full on, face first, his plans of world domination blotted out in a heartbeat. The lorry jack knifed and skidded, the driver seeing the man too late. One second the road was clear and then suddenly a man was standing there! The cab skidded off the road and stopped inches from a tree, while the back swung 180 degrees around, the chains holding the logs snapping with the pressure. A wooden sea of logs dropped off the container and hurtled down the small road. Moribund flew 30 feet through the air, landing in a bloodied heap upon the dirt track road. Somewhere inside him, he fought to get his body in shape. Somewhere inside him, he knew that a mere human lorry could not destroy him. A part of his mind knew that he would be OK, that he would rise again. His head twitched up, life returning, senses awakening, the magic mending him already, but only in time to hear a loud roaring. His eyes mended, knitted together, opened in time to see his doom. Tons and tons of wood landed on him and he screamed inwardly feeling the magic that had been keeping him alive for so long, crushed out of him, forced from him by a moving mountain of wood.

The truck driver jumped from the cab, his mind a whirling mass of panic. The logs continued on rolling across the road, before crashing into a line of trees beside the reservoir with an almighty noise that shook the earth that he was standing on. Leaves and branches fell for a few moments and dust and dirt was thrown into the air from the impact. And then silence returned. Even the trees seemed to be holding their breath. The young lorry driver saw a tangled form upon the road, a shadow of a man, and he started forward, his legs shaking and his mouth agog. He had felt the impact and seen the logs crush the man and despite the fact that he had never seen a dead person before, he knew that particular experience was about to change. His legs felt like lead, his feet hardly moving. He swallowed hard, feeling sick even before he got near the body. But then, something moved, twitched, the clothes seeming to dissolve before his eyes, the form beneath shrinking until it looked like a small pile of clothes lying on the floor. And then they too twitched and started to shrink, turning to dust before disappearing from sight before his very eyes. A blue and black shining form that billowed and contorted hovered above the spot for the briefest of moments before dispersing into the sky as if taken by an imaginary wind, a whispered shriek echoing through the trees. The man stood wide eyed in amazement and shock, but managed to get going again and reached the spot where the body had lain. Nothing remained apart from a dark outline upon the road of a figure, but not quite the figure of a man, but of something different, something that had eight tentacles rather than arms. Instinctively, he stepped back away. 'No body, just a shadow upon the road, nothing,' the man thought. He looked around at the carnage. The body had gone, he knew not how or where, the lorry was intact, the cab miraculously undamaged, the logs could be reloaded with some help. He had some explaining to do, but it could have been worse. 'Had he seen a man there?' Now he was not so sure! He peered again at the spot on the road and could hardly make out any sign at all, almost as if the mark he thought he had seen had soaked into the earth. Still shaking, the young man took a deep sigh of relief and paced back to the cab to call in.

Epilogue 2

The thing that was Moribund, the essence of the man, felt his conscience drawn back beneath the earth by a power that even he could not comprehend. Down through the solid rock, deeper and deeper he was drawn into the earth. He felt no pain, only fear of what was happening to him and where he was going. His ethereal form burst through the roof of a large circular cavern, pulled down by such force that before he could even comprehend, his essence was sucked into a large oblong jar. In an instant, a hand placed the lid on and screwed it tight.

The man stood, picked the jar up and placed it in an alcove alongside two similar size ones. Turning, he faced the centre of the room looking towards a dais set in its middle, bathed in a golden light. Upon the dais, rested a thick ancient looking book, that looked older than time itself. As he moved towards it, so the book opened of its own accord, and a page ever so slowly turned. He reached the dais and stood in front of the book. The page seemed to crash down with an audible bang. The earth beneath his feet shook momentarily, and the jars within the alcoves shook and rattled together, then settled. A thin layer of dust drifted down from the ceiling and suddenly stopped in mid-air, as the world itself, seemed to pause and hold its breath.

Golden writing started to appear upon the top of the page, written by an unseen ghostly hand. 'On this day, so the third and final age of Man, begins.'

The writing stopped, the dust settled on the stone floor and the man let out a deep breath.

"And so, it begins!" the man said looking skyward, up through the roof of the cavern towards the humans that walked upon the world, who were oblivious of the struggle that was to come, and the battles that would have to be won to save humanity.

End of Book 1

Printed in Poland
by Amazon Fulfillment
Poland Sp. z o.o., Wrocław

58705955R00075